MANHUNTER

MANHUNTER

•

Jack Lewis

AVALON BOOKS
NEW YORK

PRINTED IN THE UNITED STATES OF AMERICA
ON ACID-FREE PAPER
BY HADDON CRAFTSMEN, BLOOMSBURG, PENNSYLVANIA

This one is for Suzanne Marie;
we should have been sooner!

Prologue

Silver City, New Mexico, July 14, 1887

It was a typical July day and most folks who lived in Silver City would have thought it was far too hot a day for a bank robbery, if they thought about it at all. Maybe that's why Jake Gibson had picked this day for his big event.

Some of the storeowners had taken up the Mexican custom of closing for a few hours in the heat of the afternoon, going home for a nap, reopening when the sun was lowering toward the tops of the mountains. The ladies of the town weren't likely to be buying many ribbons or checking out the latest hat styles when they were sweaty as a black horse!

The saloons, of course, were open but quiet, and the

1

Cattleman's Savings Bank kept its regular hours, opening at nine in the morning and closing at four in the afternoon. The young man in a light-colored twill business suit looked out of place, as he strode along the sidewalk toward the bank. The gray, flat-crowned Stetson he wore showed a trace of trail dirt and a gunbelt was visible beneath his unbuttoned coat.

This man may have noticed the four horses standing hip-shot at the hitchrail in front of the bank. There was no way he could have missed the fifth horse standing nearby, its rider seeming to doze in the saddle. At the sound of boot heels announcing someone's resolute approach, the bearded rider squinted from under his hat brim, watching the young man approach the front door of the bank.

Obviously, this individual could not know that Jake Gibson and his band of robbers had taken this daily lull in activity to invade the bank and now had the bank president, Lem Turner, standing across the counter in the teller's cage with his hands raised. He had finished lunch and had sent his cashier to eat while he held down the place. Everyone in town was aware that this was the way the bank's daily business was conducted. They always said it operated like clockwork, and Turner always had been proud of that observation.

Jake Gibson and his three men all had black hoods over their faces and were hatless. It would be tough to identify them and Lem Turner was thinking about that as he stuffed bills into a canvas bag he had been handed.

"You're stallin', mister. Hurry up with that money," Gibson growled at him. He didn't see the young man in the suit come through the front door and freeze, realizing what was coming down. As the newcomer reached for his sixgun, there was a shot from the street. The force of the .44 caliber bullet drove him forward into the bank before he fell almost at Gibson's feet. Lem Turner had the nearly full canvas bag jerked forcefully out his hands. He was able to dive head first to the floor behind his counter a split instant before Gibson fired a fast shot in his direction, then stormed for the open door with the other three bandits. Lem Turner didn't move until the sound of pounding hooves told him the robbers were headed out of town.

On the sun-blanched street, the doors of two of the saloons had swung open and several men were running toward the bank. By this time, the only sign of the bank robbers was a cloud of dust that settled slowly back into the street. The interrupted drinkers crowded into the bank to find Lem Turner bending over the young man, who still clutched his unfired gun in his hand. He had been killed before he could even cock the single-action Colt. Turner glanced up at one of the onlookers.

"It's that Jensen detective, Sam," he said. "You'd best roust the sheriff outa his siesta and tell him he's needed." The onlooker, an unemployed cowboy, nodded and backed out of the door to start down the side-walk in the direction of the county sheriff's house. He glanced at the sign tucked in the corner of the bank's window without feeling any degree of irony. The sign, printed in heavy black enameled letters stated:

THIS BANK PROTECTED BY
THE JENSEN DETECTIVE
AGENCY
KANSAS CITY, KANSAS

Chapter One

Alan Jensen was happy with the way life had been going. He had just moved his headquarters from Chicago to Kansas City. The river town was thriving and had all of the social and business advantages of the Windy City. He had also found rents to be lower than he had been paying, so he had been able to take over the whole top floor of a five-story building.

But there was a more practical reason for deciding to move farther West. It was the banks in the West that were subscribing to his protective services, and he wanted them to think that he was "frontier-oriented," as he had put it to several bank presidents. He was pioneering a service in the wilder areas of the country. Pinkerton had his hold on the banks in the East, as well as the railroads, but the Southwest especially was fair game for anyone with an organization and some imagination. Yessiree! Things were looking better all the time!

Alan Jensen was a tidy-looking little man who favored spats and protected his head against the summer showers with a black fedora. His spats were black, too, sort of setting off his charcoal gray suit that he'd had tailored just before leaving Chicago. He hadn't been certain just how good the tailors farther West might be. He carried an umbrella in one hand and a black cowhide briefcase in the other, adding to his air of cityish importance.

Beside the heavy double doors leading into the building was a glass-enclosed directory. Ignoring what the other business tenants might think, there had been a bit of polite bribery to entice the property manager to list his business at the top of the array of enterprises. He paused for a moment to admire the gold lettering against a black background. This was a move that had developed into a daily habit since he had moved in. There it was:

JENSEN DETECTIVE AGENCY
We Protect The Peoples Of The West
Alan Jensen, President

"Shouldn't that be People instead of Peoples?" Tim Mathis, his lead investigator had asked the first time he had seen the listing.

"Not at all," Alan Jensen had explained. "The West

is being populated with all sorts of people. Like a lot of the big ranchers in Texas are Germans and still speak the language among themselves. The Irish came in from the East and the Chinese from the West when they were brought in to build the Transcontinental Railroad. We've got Mexicans, Indians, Jews and even moneyed Englishmen settling all over the West. These are People, yes, but they're also Peoples. Different elements of society. They'll all want a place to hold their money sooner or later. What better place than a Jensen-protected bank?"

The little speech was one he had used on several bank presidents since coming to Kansas City. Repeating it again for Tim Mathis saved a deeper explanation. Jenson admitted to himself, of course, that the motto he had incorporated might be a bit overblown, but he felt certain the day would come in the near future when that boast would be factual. He realized also that his competitors, including Pinkerton, tended to paint him as some sort of pompous fool but he blamed such accusations on professional jealousy.

Alan Jensen skipped up the four flights of polished stairs to the floor that he called his. And he expressed his feeling of well being by doing a little dance step on the hallway's new carpet as he approached his office. New carpeting in the hallway and all of the offices on this floor had been one of his demands of the building management. Having them agree and carry through had given him a feeling of major victory.

The door marked with the name of the company,

the motto and his name as president was almost at the head of the stairway, but it was Alan Jensen's habit to bypass this formal entrance, going several doors down—all of them marked *Private*—and to unlock the door to his own private office. Like lawyers, this situation allowed him to greet people in the front office, then escort them back to his own private digs. Business done, he would send them through his office door and into the hallway so that they would not return through the outer office to run into other potential customers who might be their competitors.

He had unlocked the door, shoving it open, and was in mid-step in his little dance when he saw the sole of a high-heeled cowboy boot. It was perched on a corner of his desk. Without moving, he stared at the boot sole, taking a deep breath, hoping to control his voice.

"Good morning, Jim," he declared, trying for a bass sound but only achieving a weak baritone. "I've been expecting you." That said, he edged into the room, staring at his uninvited guest as he shoved the door shut behind him.

"How'd you get in here, Barron?" Jensen wanted to know, glancing at the now closed door. He asked the question as a matter of curiosity, hiding his anger well. He didn't want any trouble that would arouse others in the building. He was building a reputation and that had to be his first consideration.

Jim Barron, he noted, was casting him an amused smile. Barron knew he was angry and knew he was working hard to hide it. He noted then that spread across his desk were several rags and parts of a dismantled .45 Colt single–action Army sixgun. There was also a can of gun oil. Barron held one of the rags and a small part in his hands.

"Get in here?" he asked lazily. "No great problem. It's amazing some of th' things you can learn up there in that Iowa State Penitentiary, if you just pay a little attention."

Jensen busied himself by hanging his umbrella on a coat hook, then sliding the briefcase onto his desk. "Like I said, I've been expecting you. They let me know when you were released."

Barron was still smiling and his tone was pleasant. Silently, Alan Jensen categorized it as dangerously pleasant.

"It took me a little longer t'get here than I'd planned," he admitted. "They don't give you much money when they let you out of Fort Madison." He offered a shrug, inspecting the gun hammer he had been polishing. As an afterthought, he added, "But I expect it ain't too much different than any other prison."

Somewhat assured, Jensen took a step closer, surveying the workings of the sixgun laid out in front of Barron. "Getting it cleaned up, huh?" Barron laid aside the hammer and picked up the barrel, holding it up to the light to inspect the bore.

"Yeah," he acknowledged. "It's pretty dirty. No rust, though."

Jenson hastened to nod, trying to smile. "That desk, my old chair you've been using and a file cabinet are the only three pieces of furniture I brought with me from Chicago. That gun's been right there in that same drawer for the full five years, Jim. Your brother cleaned it before he put it in there for me to hold. No one's ever touched it since."

Jim Barron paused, lowering the gun barrel, his pleasant smile gone. "Tim Mathis is not my brother," he growled. "He's my half-brother." He nodded toward the gun parts. "I figgered he'd start wearin' this gun himself. He won the right, I reckon."

Jensen was plainly worried by this sudden change in attitude. "He wouldn't do that, Jim. He only brought you in because it was his job. You're the one who taught him the business. Don't think like that."

Barron carefully laid the gun part on the desk and leaned back to stare up at Jensen with a cynical grin. "That's right. You sent him to bring me in, and th' minute I was convicted and tucked away in Fort Madison, he stepped into my shoes here."

Alan Jensen's anger suddenly blazed through his forced calm. He leaned across the desk to stare at Jim Barron, scowling. "Let's understand each other, Jim. Until they gave you five years for manslaughter, you were my best agent. You taught Tim everything he knew. When you were gone, he was my best agent. That's why I sent him to bring you in."

He paused for a breath before plunging on. "Tim understood one thing you didn't. Wearing a Jensen badge did not make you God with a gun!"

"The only person I shot was Ringo Smith. He was triggerin' his gun all th' way to th' ground." Barron stood up to face his accuser, matching scowl for scowl. "I fired one round, and got five years for some-one I killed accidentally!"

"You were the one still on his feet," Jensen said carefully, staring into his former agent's eyes. "And the law says any death involved in commission of a felony makes all concerned equally guilty in the eyes of the law. And the prosecution called it a duel. There's a law against dueling in Iowa. You were in-volved."

"And you fed me to th' wolves," Barron snarled. "You was so worried about th' name of your company gettin' involved you didn't even show up for th' trial."

"There was nothin' I could've done, Jim. And th' fact that you just saddled up and rode out of town after the shooting and I had to send Tim to bring you back only compounded the felony."

The two men glared at each other for a long moment before Alan Jensen forced a smile, shaking his head. "It doesn't matter now, Jim. You're out. Is there any-thing I can do to help?" He was looking the other man up and down. "You'd look a lot better in something besides that prison-issue suit. Can I lend you some money?"

Appearing almost self-conscious, Barron looked down at his thin coat, running his fingers along the lapel. "We didn't go in much for fashion at Fort Madison." There was bitterness in his tone. "I'm about five years behind on what's stylish."

"Jim, I'm still your friend. I'd be happy to stake you." Jensen was taking advantage of what he thought was an opening. Barron looked up at him, eyes narrowed in a calculating expression.

"Do you want to give me back my job, Al?" he asked softly. Jensen hadn't expected that. He took a step back and took off his hat, the other hand's fingers running fretfully through his hair. Barron's expression was one of cynical amusement as the other offered a shrug, shaking his head at the same time. When he spoke, his tone was pleading for understanding.

"I can't do that, Jim. That's the one thing I can't do." He shook his head again, looking down at the top of the desk that stood between the two of them. "We're a big outfit now. Almost as big as Pinkerton. We're a highly respected business. Our interests won't allow me to hire you back."

Barron nodded his head, acknowledging the fact that he had known the answer before he had broached the subject. "What you're really tryin' t'say is that them big banks wouldn't want you t'have an ex-con on your payroll."

Alan Jensen offered a glum, perhaps guilty nod of agreement. "You said it better than I could, Jim. I'll help you any other way I can, but I certainly can't risk the integrity of the firm by putting you back on the payroll."

Looking down, Barron began to quickly reassemble the Colt revolver. Both men were silent for a long moment before the recently released man spoke. "I shouldn't've asked th' question, Al. I knew the answer." He looked up, continuing to fit parts together automatically. "I only stopped in here for two reasons. I wanted to talk to Tim." He looked down at the gun, which was totally reassembled. "And I wanted to pick this up. Where's the holster rig?"

"In the bottom drawer." Jensen watched as Barron bent, opened the drawer and drew out the holster and gun belt, inspecting them closely.

"Well, it didn't rot, but it sure needs some oil," he said finally. He slipped it around his waist and buckled it quickly. "Doesn't look like th' Iowa State Penitentiary added any inches around my waist, at least." Without looking at Jensen, he unbuckled the belt and picked up the sixgun to slip it into the holster. Jensen leaned across the desk, frowning.

"Jim, why don't you leave the gun here? For a while, at least?" he asked quietly. Barron did not attempt to keep the cynicism out of his expression, as he glanced up at his ex-employer.

"Now, Al, you shouldn't ask a question like that.

I'm a killer, remember? What good's a man like me without a gun?" His tone was chiding, almost as though admonishing a child.

Jensen shook his head, his attitude saying that he knew he was wasting his time. "You just don't understand, Jim. Times have changed. Even in the West, we don't live by the gun anymore. The badmen are gone. The James boys. The Youngers. The Daltons. All gone. The sixgun went with them."

Barron's features had hardened during Jensen's statement. "I didn't ask for a lecture, Al. I got them right reg'lar from a warden I know. I just come for my gun."

"You said something about wanting to see Tim? You're not after him for bringing you in?" The question was tentative, as though Jensen wasn't certain he wanted to hear an answer.

Barron offered a shrug, as he laid the gunbelt on the desk. He answered with what could only be interpreted as a sad little smile. "I don't hold anything against Tim. He was doin' his job, like you said, when he came after me." There was a moment of hesitation. "And he is my brother."

Jensen reached across the desk as though to put his hand on Barron's shoulder, but the ex-con shook it off, face hard again. His voice was soft, when he spoke. "But you're not my brother, Al. By no means. And you didn't mind throwin' me to th' wolves t'protect your precious business."

Jensen was surprised, unnerved by the accusation. "You shouldn't feel that way, Jim. You know I—"

He was cut off by a sharp knock on his office door and turned toward it. Jim Barron, eyes narrowed, staring in the same direction.

"Who is it? Come in!" Jensen called. The door opened slowly for a uniformed Western Union messenger, a teenager with scraggly teeth and the hint of a blond mustache.

"Nobody in th' front office," he ventured, glancing from one man to the other, finally settling on the older man. "Your name's Jensen?"

There was a nod. "I'm Alan Jensen. That's me." He was already digging in is pants pocket for the tip he knew was expected. Barron suppressed another cynical smile. Business in the big city, he reflected. Everyone expecting a handout. The boy doffed his uniform cap and dug a yellow envelope out of the lining.

"Telegram for you, sir," he announced unnecessarily, extending it in exchange for the coins Alan Jensen handed him. "Thank you, sir. Hope it ain't bad news." As the youth closed the door behind him, Jensen stared down at the envelope, then began to tear it open. During this transaction, Barron seated the sixgun firmly in its holster, then wrapped the wide cartridge belt around it several times, securing the buckle to make a tight bundle. With it tucked under his arm, he glanced at Jensen, but the latter's attention was on the telegram

Jack Lewis

he was reading. Quietly, Barron moved toward the door through which the messenger had departed.

Jensen looked up, frowning, then saw that Barron had moved. "Jim! Wait!" About to pass through the door, Jim Barron paused to look back at him. "It's about Tim!"

"What about Tim?" Barron stared at him frowning, distrustful. He seemed not to notice that the older man's face was twisted by a combination of anger and grief.

"Silver City, New Mexico. A bank robbery."

"I thought you said things had changed," Barron snarled, his attention now on the telegram in the other man's hand. "What about Tim?"

"He's dead, Jim! Shot in the back!"

Chapter Two

Jim Barron stared at the shocked features of Alan Jensen for an instant, then grabbed the telegram out of his hand. The message was scrawled across the blank in heavy black pencil, but he was able to read it:

Alan Jensen Jensen Detective Agency Kansas City, Kansas your agent, Timothy J. Mathis, killed yesterday during bank robbery stop bandits escaped with twenty thousand dollars stop sheriff requests information regarding disposition of body of deceased agent stop Lem Turner.

Eyes narrowed, Jim Barron handed the rectangle of paper back to Alan Jensen. When he spoke, his voice was a rasp. "Who's Lem Turner?"

Jensen was staring at the telegram, again. He didn't look up as he answered. "One of our client bankers. He signed on after you left. Runs the Cattleman's Savings Bank in Silver City."

Expression a mask of hardness, Barron turned again toward the door. Again, Jensen's voice stopped him.

"Jim, wait." He hesitated for a moment, as Barron waited, staring at him. "I've changed my mind. You do have a job here."

Barron returned the stare for a long moment, grim expression unchanged. Finally, he nodded. "I'll be leavin' soon as I can catch a train."

"Be best to get off in El Paso and get a horse. You don't want to pull into Silver City on a train and have folks start asking questions." Jensen was agreeing with him, while suggesting strategy. "You'll need some money. I don't have much here and the banks don't open for another hour or so."

"I've got enough t'get to El Paso. Wire it to me in care of the stationmaster there," Barron ordered, then was struck by another thought. "I'd better have th' badge, too. At least to show to this Lem Turner, if I figger he should know who I am."

Jensen nodded agreement and walked around the desk, opening one of the drawers. He found a Jensen Detective Agency badge and held it in his clenched fist as he faced Barron.

"One thing, Jim. Like I said, times have changed. You can't handle this like you might have five years ago. We're a big outfit now. Now we have to work more with the local law."

Jim Barron stared at the other man, something mocking in his expression. "Let's get somethin' straight, Al. I'm not interested in your agency. Not in th' bank or its money. You're hirin' me t'find a killer." He looked down at Jensen's clenched hand. "Maybe you'd best keep th' badge. I'll do it my way!"

Some of the starch went out of Jensen's attitude. He opened his fingers, revealing the badge. "Okay, Jim. Your way. Take the badge."

While Jensen was talking, Barron unbuckled the gun belt that held the package together. He checked the fit of the Colt single-action in the holster before strapping the belt about his waist.

"There is one thing, Jim." He couldn't help a grim smile, as he nodded toward the gun rig that Barron now was settling on his hips. "Without a special permit, there's a Kansas City law against wearing a gun on the street." Barron stared at him for a moment, then began to unbuckle the gun belt, shaking his head. He paused to stare at his employer.

"Don't look like there's much choice with Tim except to have him buried there in Silver City," he said slowly. "Hot as it's gotta be down there right now, they can't wait till I get there."

Jensen nodded. "I'll take care of that part, Jim. You'd better find out about trains. Let me get you a check you can cash here or in Texas."

Jim Barron found that he could not catch an El Paso-bound train until four o'clock that afternoon. In spite of his wish to get moving, he welcomed the delay so he could run some errands. His first stop was at the bank, where he cashed Alan Jensen's check made out for $500. It was noted in the corner as *Expense Money*. Despite his preoccupation, Barron couldn't help smiling. Things were obviously looking up for Alan. He could remember the days when he thought he was going to have to wrestle the little man for his bi-weekly pay check. With money in his pocket, he found a gun shop, where he purchased two boxes of Remington .44 caliber ammunition. He pondered purchasing a Winchester 1882 carbine in the same caliber, but decided to wait until he reached Texas for that. It would save lugging the weapon on the train and through the city when he arrived.

It seemed as though Kansas City was attempting to forget its Western heritage. He searched the shops for typical cowboy apparel without success. Finally, a helpful salesman suggested he check an area near the stockyards. He was certain he had seen a shop there that catered to cowboys who had come in from the West with their herds.

A skinny, bald-headed old man who had the bowed legs of a one-time cowboy ran the place and looked with disdain upon the prison-issued suit Barron was wearing. It was plain he recognized it for what it was and Jim wondered whether this dried-up little salesman might not have been issued one of those suits himself somewhere back among his years.

The only clothing he had purchased after walking out the gate at Fort Madison was the pair of boots Alan Jensen had found parked upon his desk when he had entered that morning. He had spent five years wearing prison shoes, and he had hated seeing morning come each day, knowing he was going to put on the same cheap, battered uncomfortable brogans. Most convicts, he found, firmly believed the shoes were made deliberately to be uncomfortable so an escapee wouldn't be able to run far or fast if he got over the wall!

With the former cowboy's help, he picked out two pairs of denim pants and two jackets of the same dark blue cotton material. Next came four heavy-duty shirts in dark colors that wouldn't show the dirt too much, if he couldn't get laundry on a schedule. A flat-crowned black Stetson with a four-inch brim and a heavy leather belt for his pants completed his purchases.

As the clerk was totaling up the prices, he glanced at the hat several times. Finally, he ventured, "With that flat crown, you must be headed for th' Southwest. At least, some place it don't rain much."

Barron nodded, face telling nothing. "Somewhere it don't rain much," he agreed. In that instant, he realized that prison habits, including that of not venturing information, were still with him. "Got some work to do down around El Paso," he added for the old man's benefit. "Don't rain much there."

Back in his hotel room, Jim Barron changed into the type of clothing that had been his before he had gone to Fort Madison. He had to admit he felt like a different man. He opened one of the boxes of new cartridges and loaded his sixgun, then packed it, the holster rig and the rest of the cartridges in his cheap cardboard suitcase. It carried underwear, socks and handkerchiefs he had gathered earlier. He hid the Jensen Detective Agency badge in the folds of one of the handkerchiefs. The other shirts and denims went on top of the rest and he managed to get the case closed by sitting on it. He would only need it as far as El Paso, he knew. He had neglected to buy neatsfoot oil at the gun shop, so treating the leather in the gun belt and holster would have to wait until he got to Texas.

According to the schedule he received with his ticket at the train station, it would take him three days to reach El Paso, with several changes in between. There were sleeping accommodations available as far as Oklahoma City, site of his first change, but he opted to sit up with other passengers in one of the parlor cars. In all of his earlier travels for Alan Jensen, he had never had the luxury of a lying-down sleep on a train. There was no reason to start now. Knowing the time would pass slowly, he had purchased several books to help stay the expected boredom. Although he appeared calm to other passengers, he was seething inside at the time that was being wasted. It already had been several days since Tim had been killed. With each passing day that went without investigation, the chances of identifying and catching a murderer were reduced. He settled back in his green plush seat and opened one of the books.

Alan Jensen was still in his office, finishing a batch of paper work that his office assistant, Emil Warner, had brought in earlier in the day. Jensen had been pondering his decision to put Jim Barron on the case in Silver City. He had realized even before Jim's declaration that he would be more interested in finding the murderer of his brother than in running down the band that had robbed the bank. Actually, though, their respective goals seemed to be one and the same.

Jim Barron had always been an outstanding manhunter, Jensen knew. The number of felons he had brought to trial and the amount of loot he had been instrumental in returning to Jensen's clients had gone a long way toward making the little agency a player against the majors. Jim Barron's greatest fault, Jensen always had felt, was in his attitude that a dead felon was one that precluded a long and expensive trial and used up a lot of time that he, Jim Barron, should be using in rounding up other wrongdoers.

And that sort of thinking had been what had sent him to the Iowa State Penitentiary for those five years. One of Jensen's earliest clients had been a banker in a small Iowa town called Ankeny. A German farming community, it was quiet enough, or had been, until one Ringo Smith had ridden into town with several followers. They had hit all of the businesses in town, explaining that they were selling insurance against what they referred to as a "possible catastrophe."

There was crop insurance against hail damage, flooding and even fire, but no one knew what catastrophe meant and Ringo Smith and his crew of salesmen didn't bother to explain it very well. Vandalism was the word that came to mind for many of the town's citizens, after someone invaded the town's one pharmacy during the night to smash most of the bottles on the floor, leaving a mass of multi-colored congealing liquids liberally laced with thousands of unidentifiable pills. It turned out the pharmacist had run one of Ringo Smith's salesmen out of his store two days earlier.

Several townspeople bought insurance after that event, but the operator of the local livery stable did not. He slept in a room in the stable and rather bluntly stated that he could look out for the place. He almost died in the fire that broke out less than two weeks later. Six horses never made it out of the barn and their owners were asking whether there was insurance to cover the cost of their animals.

There were similar events, including a well at the edge of town that ceased to function after someone dropped several sticks of dynamite down it. It was about then that Cyrus Croft, president of the Ankeny bank, had wired Alan Jensen with an account of what was taking place. Not only was the loss of business in the town affecting banking, but he was one of those who had refused an interview with Ringo Smith. He feared for his life.

Cyrus Croft no longer had to worry by the time Jim Barron arrived in town. While on a business trip to the next town in his buggy, there had been an apparent runaway by his team. His body was found in the twisted wreckage of the broken-wheeled vehicle. There were no witnesses to the accident, of course.

Jim Barron's approach to the problem was simple. The only law enforcement officer was the town marshal, who seemed to have come down with an unidentifiable malady that had kept him in his bed most of the time since the arrival of the band of insurance salesmen. Upon arrival in town, he went to the marshal's house with a telescope he always carried in his saddlebags. Setting the scope up on a makeshift tripod in the marshal's living room, he talked the frightened local lawman into identifying the various members of Smith's gang as they rode past on their way into or out of town. Before sundown, Jim Barron had identities on all of the individuals involved.

That evening, one of the salesmen disappeared. The next night, another disappeared. On the third day, Jim Barron sent word to the Blue Dog Saloon, where the salesmen hung out. It was delivered by a farm boy to the bartender with instructions that he, James Justice

Barron of the Jensen Detective Agency, had two signed confessions stating that one Ringo Smith had personally wrecked the pharmacy, started the fire in the livery barn and was responsible for the wreck of the banker's carriage.

The note went on to state that the two salesmen had left town for points unknown. The other salesmen were free to do the same, if they chose and acted immediately. That did not apply to Ringo Smith, however. Barron's note explained that he was on his way at that moment to arrest him on behalf of the citizens of Ankeny, Iowa, for the murder of Cyrus Croft.

There had been an immediate rush for the swinging doors by the four salesmen who had just resigned. Ringo Smith spent no time in trying to reach the back door of the place, but found it covered by the bartender, who now was armed with a double-barreled shotgun with the tubes cut to fourteen inches.

"You come in th' front door, Smith. You go out th' front door." The bartender that very morning had refused to do business with one of Smith's salesmen.

Ringo Smith was an impressive type standing over six feet tall, well dressed and his black hair carefully combed for best effect. At the moment, though, he looked trapped. "I don't even have a gun," he whined. His healthy suntan was suddenly a muddy shade of yellow.

"Yes you do," the grim-faced bartender corrected.

He hated a liar, he always said. "In that hideout shoulder holster under your left arm. Now git!"

He thumbed back the hammers for both barrels. He came out from behind the bar and used the barrels to prod the self-styled sales manager toward the swinging doors. Other customers had been frozen in place during this exercise, but they now fell in behind the bartender and followed him as he marched Ringo Smith through the doors and onto the board sidewalk outside.

Smith paused for a moment, surveying the street, before a well placed boot from the bartender sent him plummeting into the street to come up against the post holding one end of the hitchrail. As he rose, he pulled the long-barreled Schofield revolver from beneath his now rumpled dirty coat. He cast a killing look at the bartender—shotgun still level and cocked—and the others standing there, then turned to stare down the graveled street. Jim Barron was approaching with long strides not fifty feet away.

Ringo Smith raised his revolver, suddenly crouching and turning sideways to make a smaller target. The hammer was already back and he pulled the trigger, the cartridge exploding. The bullet took off Jim Barron's flat brimmed hat, but he kept coming, not breaking stride, as he drew and fired a single round from the hip. The bullet caught Ringo in the upper chest, the force torquing his body in an awkward turn, as he started to fall. His finger was jerking spasmodically on the gun's triggers as he turned. The bartender was hit by one of the bullets, and as he crumpled, he pulled both triggers of the shotgun, the recoil forces jerking it free of his dying hands.

All of that had come out at the trial later. Jim Barron went back down the street, mounted his horse and rode down to the marshal's house, reporting what had happened. Then he rode out of town in the general direction of Chicago.

It wasn't until he reached Cedar Rapids, four days later and 150 miles east of Ankeny, that he saw the reward flyers posted on him outside the county sheriff's office. The Polk County District Attorney had issued the posters after interviewing witnesses of what had happened in Ankeny's graveled street. This individual, who had aspirations to fill the governor's chair, had found the almost forgotten law that stated participants in a felony resulting in death of another could be charged with murder.

Alan Jensen saw one of the reward posters that arrived in Chicago by train three days later. He soon was on the telegraph to the Ankeny town marshal, learning what had happened. It was the type of news that no doubt would be reported far beyond the boundaries of the State of Iowa.

Alan Jensen stared at the reward poster that had found its way to his desk. There was an artist's drawing—a good likeness, indeed—of Jim Barron as well as a full and accurate description. The sovereign State of Iowa was also offering a reward of $1,000 for this man described as armed and dangerous. The reward was promised for delivery, dead or alive!

Jensen felt there was no way the Attorney General could ever win such a case if he chose to pursue it, but what could turn out to be nationwide coverage would certainly make him a more prominent political figure. Jenson now regretted giving the agency badge to Barron. It would only complicate matters, if he had shown it in Ankeny. And there was no telling where Jim might be. It always had been his habit to report in by telegraph, which he had done the day after the Ankeny shootings, offering no details, simply stating that the case was concluded.

Should Jim Barron fall into the hands of the law, it was certain he would introduce his detective badge, and that was something Alan Jensen knew he could not afford. In less than two weeks, he was supposed to address a convention of more than three hundred bankers who were coming to Chicago from all across the country. Sitting there alone in his office, he saw only one course of action: Send Tim Mathis out to find his brother and bring him in. If one of his own detectives brought in what was now being identified in the press as the "company's rogue", agent he could brag about how the agency took care of its own problems. Such a claim, he hoped, would sound good when he addressed the gathered bankers.

Chapter Three

It was more than a week after leaving Kansas City that Jim Barron rode into Silver City on a black gelding that was part Thoroughbred and had proved his worth as a traveler. Arriving in El Paso after three days of stops, starts and train changes, he had bought another set of clothes and the .44–40 Winchester carbine he always had favored as a saddle gun. He then bought passage on a stagecoach that took him to Las Cruces, where he acquired the black horse, a used saddle and bridle. The horse trader who also operated the town's livery stable had thrown in a set of saddlebags and Barron had purchased a bedroll at the local general store.

His purchases complete, he had wired Alan Jensen for more money, stating that he needed $1,000. Authorization arrived a few hours later and with it the suggestion that Jensen send another agent to help him in his investigations. A return wire to the Kansas City office stated that if another agent showed up in Silver City, he would saddle up and ride on toward California where he had been headed when he stopped in Kay Cee to pick up his gun. A return telegram promised there would be no interference and Barron went to the nearest bank where he drew a $1,000 bill on the strength of the authorization. Back at the stable, he donned the black pants and shirt he had bought in El Paso, put some of his clothing in the leather saddle-bags and the rest in his bedroll.

While other train passengers were asleep, he spent part of one night working neatsfoot oil into the hardened leather of the holster and the cartridge belt. In Las Cruces, he buckled on the rig and holstered the sixgun, noting that it was well seated, but could be drawn without the front sight hanging up within the leather sheath. The old suitcase he left behind in the stable, riding out of town, his few possessions with him.

The horse trader had told him Silver City was about a hundred miles, maybe a little more, but the country, he said, was relatively flat part of the way. When he neared Silver City, he would be getting into the foot-hills of the Silver City Mountain Range, which rose to nearly nine thousand feet in the vicinity of the mining community. The trader opined, though, that the dry weather should make it easier keep on the trail.

Jim Barron wanted to reach the scene of his half-brother's death as rapidly as possible, but he had also spent enough time on other trails over the years to know he didn't want to kill his horse. The first two days, the animal worked well at an easy jog that ate up ground at what the rider estimated to be about five miles an hour. With time out for short rests, riding ten hours a day should put him in Silver City on Tuesday.

Actually, it was Wednesday, almost noon, before he rode down the main street of the New Mexican town. He had been forced to slow his pace, for the black was not used to the thinned air that came with the increase in altitude. Barron knew it would be a week or so before the animal adapted to the mountain environment.

As he rode down the main street, Barron could see that the town had grown considerably since his last pre-prison visit. There were several saloons in evidence, as well as a large blacksmith shop probably supported by repairing mining equipment. He had noticed a number of diggings along the trail, some of them being worked by their owners, while others seemed deserted. What had been a boomtown when silver was discovered had matured into a busy trade center.

Both Barron and his horse were covered with trail dust, and the first thing he did was turn the horse into a water tank that stood between a saloon and what appeared to be a dentist's office. The horse was neither winded nor sweaty and was allowed to drink its fill before the rider dismounted and led it to the hitch rail in front of the saloon. Barron realized that several citizens had paused to watch him as he had ridden down the street, but he hadn't bothered to acknowledge their interest.

Looping one rein around the hitch rail, he ducked under the pole and glanced at the name of the saloon, the Scarlet Lily, before he entered to pause just inside the door. It was comparatively dark inside and decidedly cooler than the street, he found. He looked around slowly, as his eyes became accustomed to the dim light, then walked to the bar, noting along the way that most of the men seated at tables wore sixguns. He was back in the real West, he thought. Even in El Paso he had seen comparatively few armed men on the streets and in the business establishments.

Most of the occupants were watching him as he crossed to the bar, the bartender included.

"What'll it be, mister?" he asked, as Barron placed his elbows on the polished wood surface and looked over the array of bottles arranged on the back bar.

"Just a beer, I guess."

As Barron watched, the barman drew a beer from a tap located beneath the counter and shoved it toward him. "That's a dime, mister." He hesitated, staring at the newcomer with a slight frown. "You ain't from around here."

Barron took a sip of the beer before answering. "Just rode in. Name's Barron. Jim Barron. Who're you?"

"Charlie Reese."

Barron glanced around the room. "Comfortable place for drinkin'. You th' owner?"

Reese shook his head. "I just work here." As Barron nursed his beer, the bartender moved down the bar and began to wash glasses. Five men at a poker table in the middle of the room had continued to play, but kept casting curious glances in Barron's direction. Running the game was a man dressed as a professional gambler.

"Anyone ever seen him before?" Carl Lee wanted to know, frowning thoughtfully. Jake Gibson was seated next to him, rubbing a scraggly growth of whiskers as he stared at the man at the bar. After a moment, he shook his head.

"I don't know him. In them black clothes, looks like he's goin' to a funeral." He chuckled at his own joke, but Carl Lee seemed not to see the humor. The game had come to a halt and all of the players now were watching the dust-covered rider.

"Any idea where I can get some laundry done?" Barron asked the bartender.

"Th' Widow Stern takes in some. She's th' last house south at th' end of th' street," Reese said. "You want another beer?"

Barron shook his head, reaching to his shirt pocket and extracting a bill. He laid it on the counter. Reese walked down, picked it up and started to turn to the cash register. Then he halted, staring at the bank note for a moment before turning to scowl at Barron.

"What's this, mister?" his tone was angry. "I can't change a thousand-dollar bill?"

Barron offered an amiable smile, shaking is head. "Sorry. I don't have anything smaller." Still showing anger, Reese shoved the bill across the bar toward him.

"That beer's on th' house. I don't have that kinda change."

A quiet contralto voice interrupted any further discussion. "I can change it, Charlie." Barron turned to look in the direction of the voice. The woman was dressed in a conservative high-necked dress and had a flowered hat in her hands. She appeared to have just come in from the street.

"I just came from bank. I can change it," she repeated. Holding the bill, Jim Barron walked toward her, pausing to look into her frowning face. He couldn't help offering a grin.

"How many free beers do you get with this stunt, mister? Her tone echoed a degree of spite.

"Free beers, ma'am?"

"Let me put it another way. How many bartenders have you known who can change a thousand-dollar bill for a ten-cent beer?" She snatched the bill out of his hand and turned toward the door of what obviously was her office. Barron started to follow her, but she held up a hand.

"You stay here," she ordered and slammed the door in his face.

At the poker table, Carl Lee shook his head, scowling. "That hombre's a first-class fool. Flashin' that kind of cash around town's a sure way of getting it taken away from him!"

Jake Gibson's tone was thoughtful as he said, "Yeah. You're prob'ly right." Like the others, he was eyeing the man who stared at the door for a moment, then turned to slouch against the wall, waiting. He was looking down at his feet, grinning.

The door opened a few seconds later and the woman stepped out, clutching a handful of money in her fist. Her scowl deepened as she noted Jim Barron's grin. She shoved the money into his hand.

"Nine one-hundred-dollar bills, nine tens, and ten ones." There was an instant of hesitation. "Who are you?" she demanded, as he fanned out the bills, glancing at the denominations.

"Jim Barron, ma'am. And you?

"I'm Rita Lansworth. I own the place."

At this point, Barron removed his Stetson and offered a half bow. "And a right nice place it is, too, ma'am.

"Don't forget to pay for the beer on your way out," she ordered before she whirled and retreated into the office, again slamming the door. Jim Barron sauntered back to the bar and laid down a one-dollar bill.

"I reckon I will have that second beer," he told Charlie Reese. At the poker table, Carl Lee suddenly stood up, still staring at the man dressed in black. Jake Gibson cast him a surprised glance.

"What's wrong, Carl?"

The gambler shook his head, still staring at Barron, who was nursing his beer at the bar. "You deal this hand, Jake. Leave me out."

At first, it looked as though Carl Lee was going to confront Barron, but he strode past him and went into the office, closing the door much more quietly than Rita Lansworth had minutes earlier.

"That the bill the stranger gave you?" Lee wanted to know. Rita still held it in her hand. She offered a nod.

"Yes. Why?"

"Let me see it?" Without waiting, he took the bill from her hand and held it up to inspect it closely. The girl was surprised and puzzled by his actions. Lee turned the bill over and gave it the same sort of close inspection, holding it up to the light at one point to check watermarks in the paper.

"Is there something wrong with it, Carl?" Rita's tone was one of concern. She wondered whether she had been duped by the grinning stranger. Carl Lee shook his head and handed the bill back to her.

"I just wanted to be sure it wasn't counterfeit. It's

real enough," he announced. She held the bill up to make her own inspection, eyes narrowed.

"Counterfeit?"

Lee nodded. "I was afraid Barron was trying to pass a phony bill on you, picking up good money in the change." He offered her a knowing smile. "Can't be too careful these days.

"I'd better get back to that game," he added. "And you'd better get that bill locked up in your safe!"

As Carl Lee closed the door behind him, Rita was still staring at the thousand-dollar bill and pondering the man who called himself Jim Barron. Who was he? What was he doing here?

And why did she care? That question bothered her most.

Chapter Four

J im Barron finished his beer and slid the stein across the bar. Scooping up his change, he trickled the coins into his pocket and offered the bartender a nod as he headed for the door. Carl Lee had just come out of Rita's office and stood watching him, but Barron ignored him as he parted the swinging doors and walked out into the late afternoon heat.

He recalled the bartender's directions to the home of the widow who did laundry. It was less than five blocks away. After days in the saddle, it felt good to walk a little. He led the horse down the street as passers-by paused to stare at him from the shaded wooden sidewalks on each side of the street. The siesta hour was over, apparently, and the town was beginning to come to life once more.

As Barron led the horse down the center of the graveled street, the animal kicked up little clouds of dust that hung in the air for moments before settling. The woman who said her name was Rita was in his thoughts and he didn't know why. She wasn't particularly beautiful, but there was a stateliness about her, a self-assurance that he found strangely attractive for a woman running a saloon. Throughout his travels he had been in countless saloons and gambling halls. Most of them had women, but they were there to talk customers into buying drinks and blowing their money on the premises, one way or another. Stately was hardly the word to describe most of them, Barron thought wryly. Other terms not normally used in mixed company better suited their being.

Rita Lansworth was something different. Her quiet dignity and even her anger with him at the ploy he had used to attract attention seemed to hide a sense of humor that was not common among women making their own way in the world. All the time she had been berating him, there had been an expression of amusement in her gray eyes, the lifting of an eyebrow at something said during their exchange. She was tall, maybe a couple of inches under six feet, he judged. She filled out that conservative, high-necked dress nicely. Her complexion was flawless and she appeared to wear no makeup beyond possibly a trace of lipstick.

Barron, frowning as he walked ahead of the horse,

attempted to come up with a term that would describe her. He finally had it: quiet beauty. That said it all.

A white picket fence surrounded the small house and a staked-out goat grazed in the front yard. A practical frontier means of keeping the grass and the weeds down, the length of the rope holding the halter to the stake kept the animal out of flowers that fronted the structure. There was no hitch rail, so Barron ground-tied his gelding and went through the gate to knock on the front door. He heard no movement from within and knocked again.

"Can I help you, mister?" The voice came from the corner of the house and Barron turned to locate the source. An aging woman whose white hair was not totally concealed by her sunbonnet stood there, a hoe in her hand. She was dressed in a faded gingham dress that didn't quite cover the toes of her serviceable shoes. A set of wire-rimmed glasses was perched on her nose, but she was staring at him over the tops of the lenses, attitude one of curious interest.

"Mrs. Stern?" Barron asked politely. She offered a nod.

"I've been Mrs. Stern mosta my life mister. Kin I help you."

"I hope so, ma'am. I've been on th' trail for more'n a week and the bartender down th' street said you take in washin' from time to time. I'm hopin' you can help me."

She looked him up and down for a moment before asking, "You got any clean clothes at all?"

Barron shook his head. "What I've got on's the cleanest I've got."

"Where's th' rest of it?" she wanted to know. Barron motioned to his horse.

"In my bedroll and saddlebags, ma'am."

She looked toward the horse, then back to Barron, shaking her head, a show that men were not to be trusted in such pursuits as laundry or even personal cleanliness. "Get your stuff out, while I find a sack to put it in," she ordered, then turned to enter her house. Barron retraced his steps to the street and stripped the rolls of dirty clothes out of his saddlebags, putting them in a pile just inside the gate, then untied his bed roll and unrolled it enough to drag out the rest of his trail-soiled, smelly clothing. He piled that on top of the original bundle.

"You plannin' on using that bedroll tonight, young man?" the woman asked, as she came down the bath from her front steps with a flour sack.

"Not if I can find a room at a hotel," Barron told her.

"Then strip the blankets outa that cover and I'll wash 'em, too."

Feeling a bit like a small boy following a teacher's instructions, Barron did as he had been told. "Any thoughts on a hotel?" he asked. "Looks like there're several."

"Might try th' Miner's Rest," the woman suggested, a feisty note in her words. "I kin guarantee their beds're clean. I do their sheets for 'em."

Barron hesitated for a moment before he asked his next question. He had the feeling this was not a woman to gossip, but one never knew. Finally, he made his decision.

"I'm s'posed to see a man named Turner while I'm here. Can you tell me where he lives?"

"Lem Turner? He's one of our bankers."

Barron nodded. "Yes, ma'am," he agreed. He glanced at the darkening sky. "I figger he's probably closed down his bank for th' day. I almost need t'see him tonight. It's a financial matter."

The woman had the dirty clothes sacked and led Barron outside the picket fence to point to a corner two blocks down, then offer instructions on how to find the banker's house.

"You might have more luck findin' him in his office, though. Lem's a widower, and since his wife died, he's been married to that bank," she said. "He usually works till about seven o'clock, then has his supper in the dinin' room at the Miner's Rest. You could catch him there, no doubt."

Barron thanked her and turned toward his horse. Her voice stopped him. "You kin pick up your laundry late tomorrow afternoon. You kin change in my outhouse, if you want, and I'll wash that stuff you're wearin'."

"Sounds good, ma'am," he told her, grinning. He liked the little widow. He mounted his horse, offered here a wave, which she returned and jogged back up the street toward a livery stable he had noted earlier.

His horse settled for the night, Jim Barron walked the main street of Silver City from one end to the other. Glancing at his pocket watch, he saw that it was after 6:30 and it was verging on darkness. Standing near the bank, he glanced about to be certain no one was watching him, then sauntered to a corner and turned it. The main street and the one running parallel were divided by an alley. In the gathering darkness, he turned into the alley and strode to the back door of the bank. It was marked with a small sign that read:

CATTLEMAN'S SAVINGS BANK
PRIVATE ENTRANCE

The rear office was lit, Barron noted and he stepped to the back door to knock on it. For a moment, there was no sound from within, then he heard movement. A moment later, a muffled voice came from behind the door.

"Who is it?" the voice demanded.

"Jim Barron, Mister Turner. We have to talk," the detective answered in a low but urgent tone.

"We're closed. Come back tomorrow. And use the front door!" the voice ordered.

"I'm from Alan Jensen," Barron half snarled at the offending door. After a moment, there was the sound of a lock being turned and the door opened enough for Turner to look out. He clutched a big-bored Smith & Wesson No. 3 Frontier revolver that was leveled at Barron's chest. He hesitated for an instant before swinging the door wider and stepping back. Barron cast another look up and down the alley before he entered.

Turner closed the door, then carefully laid the revolver on a corner of his desk before he turned to extend his hand. As they exchanged grips, he looked Barron up and down carefully.

"I've been expecting someone from your office," he declared. Barron nodded.

"Al Jensen wanted me to handle this personal like. I knew Tim," the detective stated. "What can you tell me about th' bandits?"

That question brought a shrug of the shoulders from the banker. "Not much, I'm afraid. They all wore black hoods and I think the one man who spoke was disguising his voice. My teller was on the way back from lunch and saw them ride out of town. He said one of them was without a hood, but he didn't recognize him. You may want to talk to Hugh Denser. He's my teller."

Barron shook his head. "Not yet. I don't want too many people knowin' I'm workin' on this."

Turner paused uncertainly, then nodded agreement. "I guess that makes sense. Is there anything else I can do to help? I sure don't know much."

"Why was Tim Mathis on his way to see you?"

"He was investigating two other bank robberies in the county. He always stopped by as a matter of courtesy any time he was close by. At least, I reckon that's why. A social call."

Barron realized the visits were by order of Alan Jensen, not out of friendship. Jensen pulled out all the stops when it came to making the client feel he and his agents had a bank's best interests uppermost in their minds. Barron suppressed an ironic twist of his lips that verged on a sneer, as he dug in his pocket and came up with a folded sheaf of bills. He handed them to Turner.

"If you have the serial numbers of the stolen bills, you might want to check these against them. There's nine hundred dollars here."

Almost reluctantly the banker accepted the money. "I'll give you a receipt for this."

Barron shook his head. "No need. I trust you. Besides it's Alan Jensen's money." He could not suppress a slight smile. "What about the serial numbers?"

"We had them on the bills of larger denominations, but my teller has the list. I'll have to wait and check these with him. Why don't you come back?"

"I'd rather steer clear of here. I noticed you have an open and closed sign in your window. If any of th' numbers match up, turn th' open sign upside down tomorrow. That'll tell me we've gotta meet."

It was the banker's turn to nod. "That ought to

work. Sorry I don't seem of much help in this robbery."

Barron's tone was flat as he stared at the banker. "I'm not lookin' for a bank robber Mister Turner. I'm after a murderer! I reckon, though, they're one and th' same. I'll say good night."

After a quick handshake, Turner opened the door to look up and down the alley. There was no sign of anyone and he stepped back to allow Barron to depart.

Barron walked several blocks down the alley, then cut back to the main drag at an intersecting street. He sauntered down the sidewalk until he paused directly across from Rita Lansworth's saloon, the Scarlet Lily. Comparing the name to what he had seen of Rita, he was unconvinced she had named the place after herself. He should have asked the banker about her. Or maybe if he didn't appear too nosey, the Widow Stern might be able to fill him in on how a woman who appeared to have been raised as a lady was running such a place.

As he neared the Miner's Rest, he was passing an opening between two clapboard buildings when he thought he heard a moaning sound. He paused, listening and heard the sound once more. Looking between the buildings, he could see nothing. The heavy shadows made the night impenetrable. Moving slowly, he ventured into the shadows to find there was a barrel blocking his way. As he rounded the barrel, a masked figure rose from within it to jam the muzzle of a sixgun against the detective's spine. Instinctively, Barron raised his hands to shoulder level.

"Jus' stand steady, hombre. I want that thousan' dollahs!" The voice was low and gutteral, close to Barron's right ear.

Chapter Five

"There ain't no thousand dollars," Jim Barron announced. "I hid most of it."

"Don't gimme that!" came the snarl.

"I hid it in my room at th' hotel. You goin' to march me through th' lobby at gunpoint to get it?" Barron tried to keep the amusement out of his tone, but wasn't certain he was succeeding.

"Where's your wallet?"

"In my left shirt pocket." Barron made a move with his left hand as though to reach for it. The movement brought a jab of the gun muzzle against his spine.

"Don't bother," was the expected order. An instant later, Barron felt the man's left hand come around his body and begin to fumble with the button that held closed the designated pocket. The button freed, the

49

holdup man's hand jerked the wallet from Barron's pocket. At the same moment, the detective felt the muzzle of the gun tilt away from his spine. Barron whirled, clamping the man's left arm with his upper arm. With the other hand, he grabbed the barrel of the threatening sixgun and jerked it free, hurling it into the darkness. The robber was hampered by his position in the wooden barrel he had chosen as a hiding place without thought of it being a potential trap. Suddenly freed, Jim Barron swung a balled fist at the masked face. The blow caught the man's chin, forcing the triangled bandana up over his eyes. As he struggled to pull the cloth down, Barron swung another uppercut to his chin. The shift of weight tipped the barrel and sent it crashing to the ground on its side, spilling the robber with it.

At that point, Barron drew his own Colt and stepped in to slash the steel barrel across the masked man's temple. Barron had expected some sort of play for the money he had flashed, but he was disappointed at the bandana face covering. He had expected his assailant to be wearing a black hood.

His eyes had become accustomed to the darkness between the two buildings and, gun still clutched in his right hand, Barron bent to pull down the bandana. He was not surprised that the man was Jake Gibson, one of the card players he remembered from the saloon. In the darkness, he felt around the ground for his wallet that Gibson had dropped. He finally found it and slipped it back into his pocket before straightening. He glanced at Gibson as the man uttered a moan and began to stir. Without a backward glance, he walked out to the board sidewalk and continued toward the Miner's Rest.

Gibson moaned again, his hand going to the temple that had been smashed by the gun barrel. Slowly, he rolled over and managed to get to his hands and knees before he saw the folded paper on the ground in front of him. He reached out to grab it with one hand, then used the tipped-over barrel as a support in getting to his feet, where he stood tottering for several seconds, waiting for his head to clear.

His hand went to the bandana that had covered his face and he muttered a curse at the realization that Barron now knew who had tried to rob him. He moved to the end of the building and the edge of the board sidewalk where there was some light from the business structures. Curious, he unfolded the rectangle of paper he had picked up.

For a moment, he didn't understand what he was seeing. Then his eyes focused on the photo of a younger Jim Barron printed in the center of the reward flier. At the top of the poster were the words:

WANTED FOR MURDER!
$1,000 Reward

In the dim light, Gibson could not read the smaller type beneath the photo, but he assumed it was a physical description of Barron and a list of his crimes. The larger print at the bottom of the flyer indicated that the reward was being offered by the governor of the State of Iowa. Slowly, Gibson refolded the paper and tucked it into a shirt pocket. In spite of the pain it created, he again went down to his hands and knees and began searching for his hat and gun.

Jim Barron was occupying a window table in the Miner's Rest restaurant, watching the street, as he waited for his order of a steak and eggs. He kept his eyes on the window and smiled grimly as he saw Jake Gibson cross the street. Obviously in pain, the would-be holdup man moved slowly toward the swinging doors of the Scarlet Lily. The detective wished he could be inside the saloon to see what took place there, but he had to be satisfied for the moment with the platter of food the young waitress set before him.

In Rita Lansworth's office, the reward poster was unfolded on her desk and Carl Lee sat in her chair, staring down at it. Jake Gibson was looking over his shoulder, reading the smaller type that described Barron. Having absorbed the printing and photo on the poster, Carl Lee offered a chuckle, looking up at Gibson with a shake of his head.

"This is the funniest story I've ever heard, Jake. You lure a man into an alley so you can take his thousand dollars and end up finding out he's a fugitive from the law! Look at that." He pointed to a specific block of type on the poster. "Look at that! Says he's armed and dangerous, wanted dead or alive. It's crazy. Or maybe it's just poetic justice!"

"Yeah, th' whole thing's a real scream," the bandit offered, expression a grimace of frustration, "but I have an idea how we can make another haul and leave this hombre holdin' th' bag!"

The laughter suddenly disappeared from Carl Lee's face and he stiffened at what he had just heard. He offered a violent shake of his head, glaring at Gibson.

"I don't want to get in any deeper than I am, Jake."

Gibson straightened and stared down at the gambler with a glare of his own. "You're already in up to your neck, tinhorn. You'll do what I tell you!"

Lee shook his head, again. "All I agreed to do was unload the money across the poker table for you. That's all—"

The gambler's declaration was cut short as Gibson's hand shot out to grab the front of the other's coat and lift him bodily out of the oak chair. The two were face to face, noses only inches apart, as Gibson stared into the other man's eyes.

"If you want that girl t'find out where you've been for the three years b'fore she give you a job, try backin' out!"

"You wouldn't tell her!" Lee's resolve was fading even as he said the words.

"Eighteen months in the state pen as a cheap pick-pocket. A fine chance you'll have with her when she hears that!"

As the taunting words seemed to echo in his ears, Lee's gaze dropped to the floor. Gibson released his hold, allowing the gambler to drop back into the chair. His attitude seemed to change to a degree, as he stared down at the gambler. His voice was suddenly softer with understanding.

"Think about it, Carl. You'll have enough money to marry th' girl and get clean outa this part of th' country. Play it right, you can even collect a bonus! The price on Barron's head! Your share of th' take plus a thousand-dollar bonus without dirtyin' your hands!"

Still not wanting to be involved, but knowing he had no choice, Carl leaned back in the chair to stare at Gibson, who had taken a seat on the corner of the desk. "Just how do you think you're going to swing this deal, Jake?"

"First off, we hafta get Barron somewhere so we can talk t'him. He'd be mighty unfriendly should I ask him straight out, but we can try a different approach. Let's see if Troy Mitchell's at the bar."

Across the street, Jim Barron had finished his supper, paid the bill, then made arrangements with the hotel clerk to rent a room for a week. That done, he walked out of the hotel and made for the livery stable, where he caught the operator returning from his own dinner to instruct his night man and to make a final check.

"I'd like t'arrange for a week's board for my horse," Barron told him, "but there are a couple of special requirements. I want him grained every mornin'. He's a good horse, but I run him sorta ragged gettin' here. Also, I need him saddled and ready to ride every mornin'. I may not take him out, but that's what I need. I'll unsaddle him in the evenin' myself."

"I can handle that stuff with no problem," the stable operator stated, wondering why this stranger wanted the horse ready to ride at any time. He also knew it was none of his business.

"What's this gonna cost me?" Barron wanted to know, reaching to his pocket for the folded bills left over from his supper and paying in advance for a room at the hotel.

"Well, about a buck a day oughta handle it."

Jim Barron nodded and sorted a five-dollar bill out of the folded greenbacks. "This should cover a few days."

"We'll take good care of him," the other promised, as Barron slung his saddlebags over his shoulder. He then clutched his Winchester rifle in one hand and the bedroll in the other, heading toward the center of town. He had gone only a few steps, rounding a stack of hay bales, when he once more felt the muzzle of a sixgun jammed against his back.

"Try what you did on Jake Gibson and I'll blow you in half," Troy Mitchell promised. Carbine in one hand, bedroll in the other, there was nothing Barron could do except stand there. Another hard jab with the muzzle of the gun caused him to stiffen. At the same time, his own sixgun was lifted from its holster.

"Move back there t'ward th' corral," Mitchell ordered. As Barron turned, he saw that a third man was involved. This individual stepped forward to lead the way around the liveryman's corral to where three horses were tied.

The third man stopped and turned to take the carbine out of Barron's hand, indicating the saddlebags and bedroll. "Drop them there," Mitchell ordered behind him. "Then get on the horse." The third man was already mounting, while Mitchell stood behind the closest animal. Without a word, Barron did as he was told and moved to the horse tied in the center. He untied the reins from the corral fence and mounted, as the third rider levered his Winchester to drive a round into the chamber.

"Where're we goin?" Barron asked conversationally, glancing at Mitchell. The outlaw nodded his head toward the third rider.

"Just follow Sid," he ordered. "Do as you're told and you may stay alive a little bit longer!"

Following instructions, Barron reined the strange horse away from the corral and fell into line single file behind the rider called Sid. Mitchell, he knew, was still behind him, no doubt with the sixgun centered on his back.

Chapter Six

Jim Barron was unfamiliar with the established trails around Silver City, but what they were following could be considered little more than a game trail that seemed to twist through the thick growth of evergreen trees. From the odor on the night breeze, he had to assume at least some of them were spruce. There was no moon and he had to be on guard constantly to keep from being swept out of the saddle by a low hanging branch. West Texas had its badlands, but this area could also get a man killed if he didn't know his way.

The horse on which he was mounted brushed close to an unseen tree trunk, the animal seemed to be trying to get him out of the saddle. A sharp twig extending from the trunk burrowed through his black trousers to stab the flesh of his lower leg. He suppressed a curse, as he made an effort to rein the horse away from such unpleasantness.

He had wondered when they ordered him aboard the horse and had not bothered to tie his hands. Now it occurred to him that the one behind him had figured he'd be so busy dodging trees he wouldn't have time for any sort of rebellion. Of course, the fact that the man at his rear also had a gun in his hand made it more obvious that this individual felt he was in total control.

Actually, Barron mused, things were moving considerably faster than he had expected. He had carried the folded poster in his wallet since his release from prison as a reminder of what he felt was an injustice. And in spite of his attempt to be pleasant to Alan Jensen when he had first visited his new offices, there was a semi-dormant resentment of the man and his tactics that probably never would subside totally.

His half-brother, Tim Mathis, had known his friends and habits well and had run Barron down in Moline, Illinois, an industrial city just across the river from Iowa. It was here that Barron had paused to pass the time with an old girlfriend for a few days. The detective had felt that once he crossed the Mississippi River and was out of the state where he was wanted, he would be relatively safe from prosecution. Tim, though, had found him and told him he should return to Des Moines, the county seat of Polk County as well as the state capital, and stand trial. Tim said he had checked with several Chicago lawyers, and since Barron had not been involved in the insurance swindle himself, the original charges had been dropped. Instead, Barron had been charged with murder based upon the fact that the state had a law against dueling. The note he had sent Ringo Smith via the Ankeny bartender had been interpreted as the challenge to a duel.

The attorney hired by Jensen to defend him was less than a year out of the University of Iowa's law school. Jensen also had seen to it that payment to the lawyer had been arranged through a Chicago bank and that his name and that of the agency were not connected to the trial in any manner. Barron had known he was in trouble when he learned of this and Tim Mathis was equally concerned. However, the trial was scheduled and there was little that could be done to change matters at that point.

The jury had downgraded the charge of murder to manslaughter, since witnesses had testified that Ringo Smith had drawn first. The fact that the bartender had been killed in the melee had been tied into Smith's death, the prosecution leading the jury to believe that particular death was born of Jim Barron's note of challenge rather than being caused directly by Ringo Smith. The manslaughter sentence had been for seven years. Good behavior had gotten Barron released two years early.

In those five years of imprisonment, Jensen had

made no effort to see him, had never written. The warden had told him that the agency owner had deposited his back pay to a trust account in a Fort Madison bank that he would receive when released.

Twice Tim had traveled from Chicago to the Iowa prison, but Barron had refused to see him. In the beginning, he had felt his half-brother should have refused the assignment to bring him in. Later, he realized that Tim might well have kept would-be bounty hunters from trying to collect the reward on his head. Letters from Tim had been trashed, never opened. At one point, Barron had wondered why he had received no mail from anyone else. Then he came to realize he had no true friends. He had never tried to make them. Other people in his life were simply acquaintances that he saw occasionally in the course of business.

Barron pondered other things during the ride, too. He wondered where Tim was buried. It had to be somewhere locally. If he ever got out of this particular predicament, he wanted to visit the grave. His thoughts kept coming back to the girl, Rita. No, not a girl. A woman. Was her saloon the headquarters for the band of bank robbers that were making this part of Arizona its personal bonanza?

The country had opened up a bit and they now were in a boulder-strewn terrain. Musing over what had happened to bring him here, Barron couldn't help but wonder whether dropping the wanted poster where it could be found by the would-be holdup man was such a good idea. It just might be the old flyer was going to help him get suddenly dead!

The rider in the lead, suddenly held up his hand for a stop and proceeded to light a sulphur match, holding it above his head and moving it slowly back and forth.

"Okay!" came a call from the rocks ahead. "Come on in."

Sid picked up his reins and the horse started to move forward. Barron hesitated, wondering what kind of hornets' nest he was moving into.

"Keep movin', Barron. Gig that horse!"

The detective tightened a spur against the animal's flank as bidden, and the mounted trio moved a hundred yards or so up the narrow trail before a dark figure armed with a rifle was semi-silhouetted against the night sky. He was atop a huge boulder that commanded a view of the country below for miles around.

"See you got him, Mitch," the guard commented.

"Yeah. This is Gibson's hard man. He seems tame enough when a gun's pointed at him," said the rider behind Barron. The detective noted the name: Mitch. The one in front was Sid. The man he'd had trouble with must have been Gibson. Until that moment, he had simply been a face.

"They're waitin' for you up there."

Again Sid signaled his horse to move out and Barron lifted the reins controlling his own mount. The three of them rounded the boulder to see a thin yellow light several hundred yards distant.

"Home again, home again, jiggity jig," refrained Sid from some otherwise long forgotten nursery rhyme. It was hardly a home, however. It was a shack that had been built from odds and ends of hand-hewn timbers and native rock by some forgotten miner. Beside the shack was a shaft dug into the mountain, but there was not enough in the way of worked out mine tailings and other rubble outside the cave-like entrance to suggest the mine had been any great success. Barron sat his saddle until the other two men had dismounted and the one called Mitch waved a revolver barrel at him. He swung down from the horse.

Mitchell used the gun barrel to signal once more, this time toward the door of the shack. The light seen earlier was shining through the single window that seemed to be devoid of any covering.

"Get in there," the outlaw ordered. "The party's about t'start!"

The steps up to the door were formed of logs stacked in ascending order. Barron found his way to the door and slowly opened it. Not until Mitch shoved the gun barrel against his spine did he enter, pausing again to look around. His eyes settled on the man seated at the table. There was a wicked bump and some blood showing on the side of his head, where Barron's gun had hit him earlier. He also recognized the blood-spattered bandana knotted around the man's neck.

"Here he is, Jake. Come along right peaceable, too,"

Mitch announced. His tone said that he had done a good job, while the wound on the side of Jake's head showed that the one Barron now took to be the gang leader hadn't done as well. Mitch pushed Barron ahead, prodding him with the muzzle of the sixgun until the detective was looking down at Jake's up-turned face. Barron couldn't resist a small smile at the damage he had done.

"I have th' feelin' we've met somewhere b'fore," he ventured.

As he lumbered to his feet, Jake Gibson attempted to laugh in what he considered a show of good nature, but it didn't quite come off. His head still hurt.

"I hope Mitch didn't get too rough with you, Bar-ron, but I thought we oughta palaver. This seemed th' best way."

Barron, trying to hide his smile, nodded. When he spoke, his tone was wryly sympathetic. "I s'pose so. Last time we met, you wasn't much given to long conversations."

Gibson stared at him, his own smile fading a bit. Then he shrugged and indicated with a nod of his head the reward poster spread on the table in front of him. He looked back to Barron, a calculating expression replacing his smile.

"I didn't know who you was then, Barron, and a thousand dollars is a lotta money." He motioned to Sid. "Bring him a chair."

The skinny outlaw grabbed a handmade stool from

the side of the room and shoved it against the backs of Barron's legs. The other man lowered himself onto the rough timber, his eyes not leaving Gibson as the other reclaimed his own chair.

"What's on your mind, friend?" he asked quietly.

"I'm Jake Gibson," the other announced, waiting for Barron's nod of acknowledgement, then continuing. "I'm gonna let you in on a chance t'make some real money. Th' Silver City Bank's gonna be robbed again. We'll make as big or better a haul'n we did th' last time."

He paused, expecting a reaction. Barron continued to stare at him for several seconds, face showing his suspicion. "And you're gonna let me in on this gold-plated affair?"

Gibson shook his head, frowning. "It ain't by choice," he declared. "Looks like I gotta do it and you're just th' man we need. A total stranger who can impersonate a law officer!"

"Law officer!" Barron could not keep the expression of astonishment under control. Gibson saw it and offered a gleeful chuckle, nodding.

"How do you figger t'do this and why the masquerade?" Barron wanted to know, suspicious once more.

"We're gonna arrange for th' good citizens of Silver City to start a run on th' bank. Ol' Man Taylor'll hafta bring in a batch of cash from other banks to pay off! That's where you come in."

"It's an idea," Barron admitted. "In th' end, it'll break th' bank. Ain't many could stand back-to-back losses like you're talkin' about."

Gibson's enthusiasm was growing as he bent over the table toward Barron. "If you can be a lawman sent down here investigate that last robbery, it'll give us an inside track. You're certain t'be told exactly when th' money is comin' in for th' payoff to depositors."

Barron affected a frown, appearing doubtful. "I don't know, Jake. You make it sound way too easy."

He dug into the watch pocket of his black trousers, digging out his gold watch, which he laid on the table. Then he dug into the pocket again. Mitchell had been standing against the wall, watching, but had drawn his sixgun once again as Barron had shoved his fingers into the small pocket.

"There's a chance this will help," Barron announced, holding out his hand, fingers bent to cover what he was holding. The others bent forward to see what he had. He exposed a silver-plated badge that carried the words:

SPECIAL INVESTIGATOR
JENSEN DETECTIVE AGENCY

All three of the outlaws stared at the badge for a long moment. Barron didn't look up as he heard Mitchell thumb back the hammer on his sixgun. His eyes were on Gibson's features which were glutted for an instant with suspicion.

"Where'd you get it?" Gibson finally asked, staring into Barron's amused eyes.

"It's a sorta souvenir," Barron announced. "I had a run-in with its owner a coupla years back."

Gibson looked relieved, leaning back in his chair. Barron heard the sound of the hammer being lowered on Mitchell's revolver and breathed a silent sigh of relief.

"You're just what we need for this job," Gibson. "You'll get an even share when we collect."

Barron was slipping the badge and his watch back into his pocket, as he shook his head with a scowl.

"You got it a little wrong, Jake. I want an even split on both robberies. This one and th' last one, too!"

"Wait a minute!" Mitchell interrupted, stepping forward.

"That's enough, Mitch," Gibson warned, still staring into Barron's eyes. After a moment, he nodded, grinning. "You'll prob'ly earn it. We got a deal!" He reached out to grasp Barron's hand.

Slowly Barron withdrew his hand. "That's fine. Who's gonna give me back my guns and guide me back t'town?" he wanted to know, attitude now strictly business.

"Sid, give him his guns. And you can show him the way back."

The sky was overcast by the time he mounted the

horse and leveled the reclaimed Winchester across the saddle. His own sixgun was back in its holster. Looking up the steps in front of the old cabin, he exchanged waves and grins with Jake Gibson. The one called Mitchell was scowling, hand clutching the butt of his holstered sixgun. As he had repocketed his watch, Barron had noted that it was not yet midnight.

Chapter Seven

The outlaw called Sid held up his hand to signal a halt to Jim Barron. They were on the edge of a plateau from which the few lights of Silver City were visible. Somewhere behind the thin clouds overhead a sliver of moon had come up and the reflected glow spread thin light across the whole valley below.

"T'ain't far from here," Sid announced. "Three miles maybe. You take that trail down th' side and it'll put you on th' level." He pointed to an indentation in the edge of the escarpment.

"I can make it from here," Barron said, edging his horse toward the end of the indicated trail. Then he appeared struck by a sudden thought. "That man Mitch. I seem to know him from somewhere. Didn't he used to have a beard?"

"Yeah,"

Sid acknowledged. "He shaved it off."

Barron was eyeing him in the darkness. "When'd he do that?"

There was a moment of silence. Sid was considering the question, showing a frown that was visible in the darkness. "You'd best ask him that," he stated flatly.

"You're right. It's not important, though." He waved a hand in farewell. "Reckon we'll see some more of each other."

Sid was already reining his horse back in the direction from which they had come. He answered without looking back. "Seems most likely."

On the rest of the ride into town, Barron pondered the evening's happenings. It seemed to have gone well enough, but there were too many jokers in the deck being played to give him any comfort.

He arrived at the livery stable and dismounted beside the corral where he had left his saddlebags and bedroll. They had apparently been undisturbed during his hours of absence. He looped the reins over the saddle horn and turned the horse in the direction from which he had come. He slapped it on the rump and the animal began trotting back toward the plateau. It would find its way back to wherever it was fed.

Barron paused for a moment, considering his options. In the dim light, he drew out his watch and held it close to his eyes. It was a few minutes after one. With a sigh, he lowered the Winchester carbine he had

been carrying and laid it on the ground beside the rest
of his gear. A broken bale used to feed the penned
horses was a few feet away and he pulled off two
flakes of the alfalfa and prairie hay mixture, using the
compacted material to cover his belongings.

He walked to the end of the business street, then
puttered around a couple of blocks to be certain no
one was following him. Satisfied, he headed for the
house owned by Lem Turner, following the directions
given him nearly twelve hours earlier by the Widow
Stern.

The house was dark and he slipped through the
shadows to reach the back door, where he began to
tap lightly. At first there was nothing, so he tapped a
bit harder. Inside he heard a board squeak, then the
door was opened a crack.

"Who is it?" a sleep-roughened voice demanded.

"Jim Barron. We need to talk."

"Do you know what time it is?" the banker demanded.

"A bit after one, but you better be ready t'listen."

The door swung open, allowing Barron to slip in.

"I'll get a light going," the banker stated, but Barron
reached out to grab his shoulder barely visible in the
darkness.

"Best not, unless you pull th' blinds," he warned.

"Maybe we better just sit here in the kitchen," the
banker said. "Chair's next to you on the right, if you
can't see it. Sit."

Barron reached down, clutched the back of the chair and slid onto the seat. He found he was at a round table. Across from him, another chair was pulled out and there was a slight groan as the banker took a seat.

"You'd better tell me why you're here," the banker grumped, "or I may have the town marshal get you committed as mentally incompetent."

"You're banks goin' to be robbed, again," Barron informed him. That brought a mild curse from the darkness across the table.

"How do you know that?" the banker demanded.

"B'cause I'm helpin' with the robbery!"

There was another curse from the banker, this one less mild. Barron began to relate what had happened to him during the night.

"But why do I have to let them rob my bank, again?" Lem Turner wanted to know, anger in his tone. "Why can't you and the marshal arrest them, instead of playing their game?"

Barron said nothing, waiting for the banker to continue, which he did.

"Haven't they admitted to you they robbed me and killed your agent? That's what you just said. What more do you need?"

This time, Turner's questions demanded a reply. Barron heaved a sigh and spoke quietly to the distraught man facing him in the darkness.

"First off, it's strictly my word against theirs," he reminded. He also realized that in a trial, his own past as an ex-convict would be revealed. His testimony would then be considered worthless. That was something the banker didn't need to know.

"I'm also fairly certain Jake Gibson ain't runnin' this outfit, Mister Turner. He just plain ain't smart enough. He doesn't even think on a big enough scale t'come up with th' kinda plot I heard tonight."

"I'm not sure I understand what you're saying." Some of the anger and frustration had gone from the banker's voice. Now he sounded confused and puzzled.

"Give Gibson a bit of thought," Barron urged.

"I only know the man by sight," Turner protested.

"Jake Gibson tried to hold me up b'cause he thought I was packin' that thousand dollars." Barron offered a shake of his head to emphasize his point before he realized the man could not see him. "It's not like a gang leader to take on that sorta job by himself. It's th' stunt a petty thief, a small-timer, would pull to get some extra cash!"

The banker was silent for a moment. Apparently the clouds had parted outside and filtered moonlight now was filtering through the kitchen window. Barron could see the dim outline of the banker now. Turner shook his head, scowling and staring down at the oil-cloth covering the table.

"I don't know what's happening in this country, Jim. It's been a nice place to live and do business. Been that way, at least, since the last Apache troubles more than fifteen years ago. Now it sounds like we've got all sorts of badmen taking over our streets!"

"It can happen," Barron agreed. "It's sort of like a disease that has t'be stamped out b'fore it gets a good hold. I've seen it happen in other towns." Then he raised a hand as a gesture of reassurance.

"It may not be all that bad, though. I'll keep lettin' you know what's goin' on." He rose from the chair and glanced toward the kitchen door. "I'd best find th' hotel and hope not too many people see me along th' way."

The banker offered a grunt. "The only folks you'll see out there this time of night are those too drunk to find their way home!"

Barron hesitated, grasping the back of the chair, looking down at the banker with a scowl. "I do have a question, Mister Turner. How is it Rita Lansworth runs a saloon? She seems a bright, respectable lady."

The banker looked up at him, offering a nod. "I'd say she is. In fact, a lot of the ladies in town would say the same thing if you asked them."

"But why?" The question was insistent.

"Well, old Custis Lansworth come in here right after the Civil War more than twenty years ago. He was a widower with a small child and a small bag of gold. He bought the lumber at one of the sawmills and built the Scarlet Lily with his own hands. Rita was just a tyke then and we all took a liking to her.

"It took Custis most of a year to build the place.

When he finally opened, it was with a few bottles of whiskey and an honest poker game he dealt himself. He ran a clean place. No painted ladies and he'd throw a card sharp in the street the minute he spotted them."

"What about Rita, though?"

"She was always close by when Custis was building the place, using sawed off bits of lumber for toys. Once he opened, though, it was the Widow Stern looked after Rita mostly. As soon as Custis could afford to hire bartenders, he was able to spend more time with her. Bought her a pony and they'd take long rides together. They were in church every Sunday, too." The banker shook his head, with a wry grin.

"When she was about 12, Custis sent her off to some boarding school in the East. Connecticut, I think. When she graduated from there, she went on to college. It wasn't easy for Custis to run a class operation and finance that sort of learning, I'd bet. Then when he died a couple of years ago, we all figured Rita'd stay East and sell. Instead, she came in on the stagecoach and announced at the town council meeting that same day that she was going to run the place herself. She still insists on the bartenders pouring an honest drink and she sees to it that the games stay honest. She's still in church every Sunday, too." The banker paused, then added, "That's pretty much it."

"Well, it doesn't sound like she'd be th' one to head up a gaggle of bank robbers," the detective admitted thoughtfully. He had been gripping the back of the chair, listening. Now he straightened and extended his hand in the dim light.

"We'll be talkin'," he promised as they shook hands. "No match up on those bills I brought you?"

"Nothing so far," the banker said.

"There is one other thing more," Barron added, making it sound like an afterthought. "I put Gibson to a little test. Told him I wanted a share of both robberies. He agreed real quick like."

The banker shook his head. "That doesn't sound likely. What's it mean?"

"He plans on killin' me when he's got th' new money in hand!"

There was a sound at the window and Barron whirled toward it, sixgun suddenly appearing in his fist. He fired once and the sound of the shot was echoed by broken glass falling onto the bare wood of the kitchen floor. The sound of scrambling feet was also audible.

Barron leaped to the window and used the barrel of his revolver to sweep away the shards of glass still held in the frame. An instant later, he clambered through it. Landing amid some rose bushes, he was in time to see a figure race around a corner. Barron was on the point of triggering another shot, when the window blind in the house next door was suddenly raised, rattling around its spool. Barron whirled toward the new sound, sixgun cocked.

The light coming from the window revealed Rita

Lansworth, a gown over her shoulders. She was glaring at him, as Barron lowered the muzzle of the revolver.

"What're you doing out there?" the woman demanded.

"Just testing my gun," Barron replied, airily. Considering the situation, he thought it as good an answer as any. The glass window had been open. Rita Lansworth slammed it down, locking it before she fought with the shade for a moment and lowered it with a vicious snap.

Barron holstered his gun and glanced up at the banker who was looking through the broken window.

"You didn't tell me she lived next door."

The banker offered a shrug. "I hadn't gotten to that part, I guess." The detective raised his hand in signal that the excitement was over, then moved between the two houses to the street.

On the way to the hotel, he detoured past the stable to gather up his carbine, saddlebags and bedroll. The moonlight was dying, faded by a hint of dawn in the East, as he strode through the lobby of the Miner's Rest and found the room he had rented in the afternoon.

Stripping off his sweat-encrusted clothing and boots, he slid between the sheets to stare at the ceiling. In several hours, the tale of his firing a shot between the homes of the banker and the saloon owner would be all over town. A lot of people, including Jake Gib-

son and who ever he was working for, would want to
know why.

Finding out and proving who had killed his brother,
he mused as he closed his eyes, was turning into a real
bucket of snakes!

Chapter Eight

Sometime after daylight, Jim Barron awoke. It was cloudy again, he noted through the window opposite his bed. There was light but no sign of the sun. Without resorting to his watch, he judged it to be about six o'clock. He also reasoned that there was no reason for him to rise, since he'd been up for nearly twenty-four hours before he had finally reached his bed.

He lay there for a moment, pondering the happenings of the night that had just passed and realized that he had been too tired for common sense. If that had not been the case, he would not have fired the shot at whoever had been near the window. For all he knew, it could have been some passing drunk smitten with Rita Lansworth, up to a bit of Peeping Tom—foolishness. However, the man had not run like a drunk. Bar-

78

ron punched his pillow into a fluffier mass and turned on his side to face away from the growing light and shut his eyes.

In the Scarlet Lily, Charlie Reese had set the chairs up on the tables and was directing the swamper in mopping the floor. The old man, white-haired and bent from labor in the mines, earned a few dollars a week for swabbing out the saloon every day before dawn. Down the street, at one of the restaurants, he earned three meals a day washing dishes and keeping the place clean after hours.

"You missed a spot over there at the end of the bar," Reese growled, pointing toward the area in question. He didn't know why Rita kept the old man on beyond the fact that he had worked for her father, doing the same chores. Of course, the old miner had been younger then, moved faster.

Answering with nothing beyond a frustrated shake of his head, Ben Stover moved the bucket toward the end of the bar with his foot, dipped the mop in it, then wrung it out with his hands. Muttering to himself, he began to swab the spot Charlie said he had missed. They both knew he had covered it when he first started.

Reese looked up as the door to Rita's office opened and Carl Lee staggered out. He stood there for a moment, weaving back and forth. It was obvious he had been asleep, but he was still showing the effects of alcohol. Reese eyed him with an expression of disgust.

He had known Lee was asleep in the office that he had not gone to his room at the hotel. He had let the gambler be, not trying to awaken him. Now, as Lee made his way to the bar, Charlie walked toward him.

"You shouldn't be drinkin' like this, Carl. I thought you went t'bed."

"I need a drink," Lee muttered, leaning against the bar and surveying the array of bottles a few feet away.

"I'm makin' coffee right now. Better have some of that. Try t'get sobered up."

"Just gimme a drink," the gambler insisted. He pounded on the wood as he said it. Reese shrugged and went behind the bar, handing him a shot glass and a bottle. Three men entered the room. They paused, observing the play between gambler and bartender. The two of them made an interesting study in opposites. Reese was well over six feet and muscular. He was in his forties and his face showed the effects of hard living. Carl Lee, on the other hand, was at least four inches shorter and slight of build. In his mid-twenties, his face was handsome to the point of appearing almost feminine. The two of them looked like David and Goliath. One of the newcomers shook his head.

"Too bad," he muttered. The other two men nodded. One had the appearance of a rancher, while the other two had the look of local businessmen. One of them, Paul Slade, was the local mortician as well as the county coroner.

"The coffee ready yet, Charlie?" Slade called across the room. Charlie Reese looked at him and nodded.

"Should be by now. I'll take a look." Reese moved behind the stretch of polished mahogany, until he reached a door near the end of the bar and disappeared. A minute or so later, he reappeared with a metal tray bearing three steaming cups, a bowl of sugar and a small metal pitcher.

"Don't have no cream yet this mornin'," he warned, "but there's canned milk in th' pitcher." The three muttered their thanks as he laid the containers out before them, including three tin spoons. Straightening, he headed back to the bar. Carl Lee had turned and was leaning against the bar, eyeing the three coffee drinkers.

"Carl, go on back to th' hotel and get some sleep," Charlie suggested, almost begging. "When Rita finds out you closed down th' table last night so's you could get drunk, she ain't gonna like it a bit!"

Lee's eyes still were on the three men at the table. If they looked closely at his eyes, they might have surmised that perhaps he was not as drunk as he let on.

"There ain't no money to be won in this town anyway," he declared, scowling. "No one's got any loose money since Turner's bank got robbed."

Charlie Reese cast him a dubious glance as he worked behind the bar, apparently cleaning up what the night man had left undone. "I can't see how a robbery'd make everyone poor all of a sudden."

The gambler turned suddenly to rest his elbows on the bar and cast Reese a knowing sneer.

"Ol' Man Turner can't pay off half his accounts, if folks start asking for their deposits," he declared. "He's smart. He's keeping quiet, so they won't know how shaky his bank really is after being cleaned out!"

Charlie Reese quit working and had straightened to stare at the gambler. At that moment, a bald-headed man entered from the street and paused to speak to the three men at the table. Charlie spotted him immediately.

"Zeke, you're gonna have t'take over here for a time," he announced. The bald-headed Zeke turned to glare at him.

"Come on, Charlie, it's Sunday. I didn't get outa here till three o'clock. I've been for a long walk and took a bath. Now I want my breakfast b'fore I get some sleep!"

"It won't be long," Reese promised. He was already moving, pulling a coat off the hatrack at the end of the bar and shrugging into it. As he passed Carl Lee, he stopped to stare at him, eyes narrowed.

"Sure hope there ain't nothin' in what you say about th' bank bein' broke. My money's comin' out th' minute Lem Taylor opens up!" The three men at the table seemed to have forgotten their coffee. They had been listening and now exchanged disturbed glances.

As Charlie reached out to part the swinging doors, Rita Lansworth pushed in from the opposite side. He nodded to her.

"G'mornin', Miss Rita. I'll be back soon." He didn't stop, pushing through the doors, his heels pounding on the board sidewalk outside as he strode away. The woman, however, was staring at Carl Lee, who stood against the bar, shot glass in one hand, bottle in the other. He saw, Rita and raised the tiny glass in salute.

"Good morning, ma'am. I trust you had a good night."

Scowling, she stopped before him. "Better than yours obviously." Her hands were on her hips and she glanced down at the glass and bottle clutched in his fingers. "What are you doing here in this condition? You know my rules!"

Carl Lee only grinned at her self-consciously, the erring boy caught in mischief by his teacher. "Condition? I'm in good condition." He spoke slowly, forming his words as only a drunk will do. "Best condition I've been in for years!"

Trying to ignore what was going on, Zeke had removed his coat and hung it on the hat rack before he moved behind the bar. Rita looked at him.

"I don't want him around here, Zeke. He needs to sleep this off."

Zeke offered a shrug, not wanting to be involved. "You could put him in your office."

"No. Not there. I'll walk him down to the hotel."

This had happened before, but it had been more than a year ago.

Carl Lee stood erect, grinning at her, still wavering. "You're going to walk me? That's nice. Been a long time since you did that." He started for the door, half stumbling, as Rita hurried to catch up with him, grabbing his arm. She removed the bottle and glass from his hand, setting them on a table, then took the same arm to navigate him through the swinging doors.

At the table, the coffee drinkers watched them leave. The rancher turned to look at the others, face creased with a frown of worry. "You take any stock in what he said about Lem Taylor not bein' able t'pay off depositors?"

One of the others shook his head, his own frown deeper than the one he was looking at. "I don't know, but I heard th' same sort of stuff last night at th' restaurant. Not much we can do today. It's Sunday, but I'm gettin' my money in cash soon as he opens tomorrow mornin'!" The speaker kept his voice low so the bartender would not overhear. The third man nodded agreement.

"Don't hurt t'be careful in times like these," he muttered, "but we'd best keep it quiet till we get our money. I don't want t'be standin' in a long line with nothin' but disappointment at th' other end."

Carl Lee managed to maintain a relatively sober appearance as he crossed the street and made it into the Miner's Rest, Rita guiding him and talking encouragement. He had become sullen and silent and had concentrated on putting one foot ahead of the other.

The desk clerk was on duty and looked up, frowning at what he saw. Lee was out of steam and began to stagger, dragging down the girl. She looked at the clerk with a pleading expression.

"Help me, please. He needs sleep!"

There was only a moment's hesitation before the clerk grabbed a pass key off a rack. He didn't want to go through the pockets of a falling-down drunk to find the man's key. Coming out from behind the desk, he got one of Carl Lee's arms over his own shoulder, clutching the gambler's hand to hold him in place, his other arm going around the body.

"Okay, Carl. Let's take it easy on the stairs now," he said gently, taking a step that Lee tried to match. One step at a time, they made it up the steps and down the hallway, Rita following a yard or two behind. The clerk had the pass key in the fingers of the arm that was around Lee's back to support him. He held it out toward the woman.

"Here's the key. Open up for us."

Rita opened the door quickly, pushing it wide. The clerk half carried the now staggering man into the room and lowered him onto the bed, lifting his legs to get them off the floor.

"Thank you," Rita said, trying to smile, as she handed back the key. "I'll take care of him now."

The clerk cast the drunk a glance of disgust. "My

name's Beatty, Miss Lansworth. Any problems, just step out in th' hall and call. I'll hear you." As he closed the door, he noted that the drunk was trying to sit up on the edge of the bed.

Rita watched him go, a wry smile touching her lips. Joe Beatty was new in town. She hoped he didn't know enough people that he'd say much about her staying in the room with Carl. Gossip, she had learned long ago, was any small town's chief entertainment.

Carl Lee had managed to get to his feet and launched himself across the room, grabbing Rita by the shoulders to keep from falling. "Jus' one kiss b'fore you go," he slurred. In the back of his mind, he knew he was totally drunk. It had to be that last few drinks he'd had at the bar. He bent toward the girl, offering a loose-lipped grin of anticipation.

"Stop it, Carl. You know better!" If a lady was able to snarl, that was what she was doing, she realized. She shoved him backward, propelling him on loose legs to the edge of the bed, where he collapsed across the mattress.

"What's happened to you, Carl? You said you had quit drinking. What happened?" There was a beseeching note in her voice, but as Carl simply sat there, rocking back and forth, staring at the floor, some of her anger returned.

"You used to be a man, but you've changed!" she charged. The gambler slowly raised his head to look at her, his drunkenness glazed by the softness of misery. He shook his head, mumbling.

"Man? Changed? I haven't changed." He shook his head again. "Neither've you. Jus' like when we were kids . . ."

"What're you babbling about?" Rita wanted to know, staring at him. Carl was looking past her, though, showing a smile of something pleasant but a long way off.

"Jus' like when we were kids. Little Carl stubs his toe and falls in the mud. Rita's always there to pick up the pieces." His words were a monotone and he glanced about uncertainly, then rubbed his hand across his eyes. He slowly sank back on the bed, eyes closing. Rita stared at him, scowling, then her expression softened. She crossed to raise his feet and settle them on the bed. She closed the door softly, as she left, only to find herself face to face with Jim Barron. He had just locked his door across the hallway and was buckling on his gun belt as he looked up to see the woman glaring at him.

"Getting ready to storm into someone else's bedroom with a gun?" she asked. Barron seemed to ignore her as he eyed the door through which she had just come.

"Who's in there?" he wanted to know.

"I don't think it's any of your business, but it's Carl Lee. He works for me."

"I want to talk to him," Barron grated. "Now."

Rita half turned to open the door, allowing him to look in.

"Not now. He's passed out." She paused for an instant. "Why do you need to talk to him?"

"I'm a detective," Barron told her. That was the role he was supposed to play for the bank robber band. There was no harm in letting it be known now. "And I apologize for last night. I was talkin' with Lem Taylor and someone was listenin' at the window. I took a shot at him, but he got away."

"And you wanted to check Carl Lee for bullet wounds?" she asked. "He's whole and in one piece physically. He just needs to sleep it off."

Barron touched the fingers of his right hand to his hat. "Sorry t'have bothered you, ma'am. Again, my apologies for last night."

She watched as she strode down the hallway and took the stairway to the lower floor. Then she turned and locked Carl Lee's door.

Chapter Nine

Jim Barron was seated near the window in the hotel restaurant when he glanced through the doorway that joined the eatery with the lobby. He watched as Rita Lansworth crossed the lobby, then he concentrated on the window as she walked out of the hotel and paused for a moment on the board sidewalk. Up the street, church bells were tolling a call to worship and she turned toward the sound. It was then he realized it was Sunday.

The other thing Barron noticed was a gathering of citizens in front of the Cattleman's Savings Bank. He pondered this, as he ordered breakfast, then settled back in his seat to watch the assemblage continue to grow until there were probably twenty people in front of the bank. Gathered in small groups, they seemed to be engaged in nervous conversation, some gesturing toward the front door of the bank.

Since his late night meeting with Lem Turner, he had taken his horse out of the stable to retrace part of the trail to the gang's hideout, checking out various landmarks so he would know his way if he had the next time he had reason to find the hideout. Jake Gibson and his gang had been steering clear of town from what Barron had seen.

The waitress brought his order of steak, eggs and toast and bent to replenish his coffee. When she glanced at him to determine whether he needed anything more, he nodded to the window.

"What's goin' on down there in front of th' bank?" he asked. The heavyset woman frowned and shook her head.

"Don't know. But I see folks there I thought'd be in church."

Barron looked back to the street, trying to determine whether Rita was in the crowd. He had assumed she was on her way to church. He felt a sense of relief when he couldn't spot her. He finished his coffee, wondering why he should be bothered.

Barron paid for his breakfast along with a tip before he stepped out into the growing heat of the morning. In spite of the later hour at which he had found sleep, he felt alive. The visit to Jake Gibson was probably responsible for that, he knew. Things were starting to happen.

A cowboy who looked like he was headed toward the Scarlet Lily came down the sidewalk toward him and Barron raised his hand in signal. The young man, no more than 20, glanced at him curiously and halted.

"What's goin' on down in front of th' bank?" Barron asked. The cowboy looked back in the direction from which he had just come and shook his head.

"I don't rightly know. Some talk about the bank goin' bust and th' banker holed up inside to keep 'em from lynchin' him!"

"Lem Turner's in the bank?"

The cowboy offered a shrug. "That's what I heard someone say, mister."

"Thanks." Barron was already making his way down the street, but instead of approaching the bank from the front, he circled and came up to the rear door. He knocked on it and waited. Nothing happened and he knocked again, drumming knuckles in an insistent message.

"Come on, Turner," he finally called in a low voice. "It's Barron. Let me in!"

With his usual caution and a gun in his hand, Lem Turner pulled the door open a crack. Recognizing the detective, he opened the door then slammed and locked it.

"You picked a lousy time to call," he offered sourly. Barron could hear the pounding on the front door and the angry voices. "What can I do. That crowd's getting mighty riled."

"I don't think you have much choice," Barron said. "You have to go out there and face them. Tell them you'll be open tomorrow morning as usual. But you'd better get to that telegraph operator and round up some money quick like.

"Also, you'd better have them wire you back that the other banks are lending you money to cover. You're not going to have that much ready cash in the morning, but those telegrams should prove you're working out the problem." Barron was struck by another thought. "They could wire you the funds, but that ain't cash. You've gotta have it brought in either by messenger or stagecoach."

"That might work," Turner said slowly, thinking about it. "Most of those folks out there are my friends. Or I thought they were."

"Money's come between a lot of friends down through th' ages," Barron offered. "I reckon it started with thirty pieces of silver. Maybe even b'fore that."

"Come back me up so they don't try to rush the door," Turner said. "I'm going to have to tell them who you are."

"That seems to fit into Jake Gibson's schedule," Barron offered, as they both moved toward the front of the bank where business was conducted. Someone had thrown a rock through the square of glass in the front door. Next, they both realized, it would be the big plate glass window emblazoned with the name of the bank.

The rumble of voices could be heard plainly, and the banker stopped, listening with a worried, fearful expression.

"Come on out, Turner. We know you're in there," someone called.

"Yeah. Afraid t'come out and face us?"

"Maybe he's sackin' up the rest of our money so he can skip town!" another voice suggested.

Turner shook his head, staring at the hole in the small window. "I don't know, Barron." His voice echoed his fear. "I don't think they'll listen to me."

"If you don't talk to them, they'll come in and drag you out. The longer it is, th' madder they're goin' to get." Barron hesitated for an instant, then reached in his watch pocket and pulled out the Jensen badge. He pinned it on his shirt pocket.

"I'll open the door and sorta introduce you," he offered. "Maybe th' surprise'll shut them up for a minute."

"Yes. That might work." The frightened banker was looking for any means of avoiding a confrontation. "You talk to them first."

Barron nodded and stepped to the door, unlocking it. Several people tried to force their way in, but he shouldered them back, stepping out to the board sidewalk. The surprised citizens made room for him, puzzled by this development. They also saw the badge.

"Folks, I'm a bank detective. Name's Jim Barron." He looked around at the crowd, almost doubled in size since he had come in the back way. "I'm here to see that this mess gets straightened out and th' bank recovers the holdup money."

There were mutterings of disbelief from some of the onlookers, but others plainly wanted to hear more.

"I think it's time you hear what Lem Turner has to say," Barron went on, offering them a smile. "He'll do it better if he's sure none of you has a hangman's rope!" That brought chuckles from the crowd. Barron noted that on the far edge of the gathering, Jake Gibson and his gunman, Mitch, were listening. The detective turned to open the door and waved Turner out. The crowd started to rumble again, but Barron held up both hands in a plea for silence.

"Folks, Mister Turner's goin' t'give you th' facts of what's happenin' and what he's doin' t'solve th' problem." There were rumblings, again, and he increased the volume of his tone. "Being robbed is just as big a problem for Lem Turner as it is for all of you. Try to work with him for a few days." He turned to nod at the banker, who tried to hide his fear as he stepped forward.

"I don't know who started the rumor that we're busted," he said, "but it's not true. What is true is that the bank does not have the funds to pay off all of the depositors today." Before the rumblings could resume, he held up his hands, asking for silence.

"I'm arranging to borrow money from a bank in Albuquerque and another one in Carlsbad. To do this,

I'm going to have to pledge some of the mortgages I hold on the properties some of you own. In fact, I may even have to sell some of those mortgages at a discount to come up with the money."

"You mean you're gonna sell my paper to some banker I don't know?" one elderly man asked.

"I may have to, Jonas," the banker replied. "It's done all the time in the big cities. In most situations, a mortgage is a negotiable security."

"This ain't no big city," the elder complained. "I had a thousand dollars in your bank. Maybe it's lost, but my mortgage is for six thousand. I wanta know who I'm dealin' with, Lem."

"It's going to be several days—three, maybe four—before I can get the cash in here to pay off depositors," the banker explained, surprised that he had found an ally, no matter how reluctant. "Frankly, I wish you'd all leave your funds on deposit, but it is your money and I'll be able to pay off, when the cash arrives."

The banker hesitated for a moment, then glanced at Barron. "I've got to get back to work," he stated so all could hear. "Jim, take over, please." He retreated through the open door and closed it.

"Okay, folks," Barron announced loudly. "You know where you stand and what's being done. Let's break it up and go home. After all, it's Sunday."

"What happens if Turner packs up the rest of th' cash and runs." It took no effort for Barron to identify the speaker as Mitch, who was standing beside Gibson.

"If that happens, I'll be ten minutes behind him with a sixgun in my hand!" Barron brushed a hand across his badge, forcing a laugh to indicate how ridiculous the question sounded.

The crowd began to break up, moving away in different directions. That was when Barron noticed that others were coming from the church, services ended. Rita Lansworth was on the sidewalk in front of the general store, watching him. He wondered how long she had been there, how much she had heard.

He raised his hand to her and she lifted her right hand a bit to acknowledge the signal before he turned and reentered the bank. When he looked back through the broken window, she was still standing there.

Lem Turner led the way back into his private office and indicated a chair in front of his desk. Barron took it as the banker settled in his own chair.

"That worked out better than I expected," Turner acknowledged. "You're quite a talker."

"Sometimes its easier to talk your way out of trouble than t'fight your way," Barron offered. "You'd best get them telegrams written and get them on th' wire so th' banks have them first thing in th' mornin'."

"I'm going to get on that right away." He cast Barron an inquiring look. "Anything else?"

"I'm curious about this Carl Lee. What do you know about him?"

The banker pondered for a moment before replying. "Not much. He showed up here a bit over a year ago. Seemed down and out, but it turned out he and Rita had known each other at the boarding school back East. She gave him a job as the house gambler and he's been at it pretty much ever since."

"He an honest dealer?" Barron wanted to know.

"If he wasn't, Rita wouldn't have him there. She's happy with the house odds just like her father was. The house doesn't have to cheat to win in the long run."

Taylor paused, frowning. "He did go on one big three-day drunk right after he got here, but no trouble since. You thinking it could have been him outside the window last night?"

Barron nodded. "Someone was there, but with th' window shut, there's no tellin' how much he heard. That was pretty thick glass and we weren't talkin' very loud."

"You don't think you hit him when you shot?"

Barron shook his head. "I didn't figger t'hit him. Just wanted t'scare him. If it was just some drunk wanderin' around and I killed him, your town marshal'd have me polishin' his iron bars by now."

The banker chuckled at the idea, then grew serious again. "I hope whoever it was didn't hear anything. You have to admit having someone visit a banker in the middle of the night's not a normal thing."

"If someone finds me with a bullet in my back, you'll know whoever it was heard too much!"

Chapter Ten

The morning had passed rapidly and Jim Barron didn't have to look at his watch to tell it was well after noon when he finally emerged from the bank through the front door. He was not surprised to see Mitch lolling in front of the Scarlet Lily, keeping an eye on the bank—and on him as well.

He wondered whether it might have been the gunslinger who had been listening outside Lem Taylor's window, but discounted the idea. Mitch was the type who would immediately return fire if someone shot at him!

Barron strode toward the Miner's Rest, then changed course. He continued walking instead toward the edge of town until he reached the Widow Stern's white picket fence. He turned in and noted that the goat had cropped down one patch of grass and had been moved to another area that was in need of mowing or, in this case, eating.

It was a warm afternoon and the front door was open, although a screen defended against flies and other vermin. Barron knocked on the door frame, and a moment later, the pioneer lady was framed in front of him.

"Mister Barron! I was just thinking about you." She smiled at him, and opened the screen so that he could enter. "I heard what happened down at the bank. Mad as some of them folks was, it was some kinda miracle, calmin' them down th' way you did."

Barron shook his head, pleased at the words by trying not to show it. "No miracle. All I tried t'do was talk common sense. Most of them understood."

The widow was reluctant to give up her evaluation. "Well, I've never seen no one handle a mob like that b'fore." Then she changed tack. "You're here about your laundry."

"Yes, ma'am." He looked down at the stained, sweat-stiffened shirt and trousers, shaking his head. "This stuff's so stiff it probably could walk by itself. I was hoping—"

She cut him off. "All of your stuff is clean, Mister Barron, but I still have two shirts to iron. I'd have them done, too, if I had skipped church. I don't do that, though. The way thing's have been goin', this town needs all th' prayers th' good Lord can handle."

She hesitated for an instant before adding, "I usually send range riders out to th'outhouse t'change, but I don't think I hafta worry about you. You can use my bedroom." She turned to lead the way, pausing to point to the room in which he could see the corner of a bed. "Wait here," she ordered.

Instead of entering the room, Barron stood with his back against the door jamb, waiting until the lady returned with clean shirt, pants and his denim jacket, all of them ironed to perfection. On top of the folded pile was a pair of clean stockings.

"This'll take care of you for th' moment," the woman declared. "Give me what you've got on and I'll wash it and it'll be with the rest of your stuff tomorrow. Okay?"

"Sounds good to me." Holding the folded clothing against his chest, he stepped backward into the room and allowed her to close the door.

A few minutes later, he emerged with his dirty clothes in a rolled bundle. "Missus Stern," he called. Somewhere a voice answered him, although he couldn't make out the words. He called, again, listening.

"Th' backyard!" was the muffled reply.

Rather than traipse through the kitchen, he found the front door. Still clutching his bundle of dirty clothes, he circled the house and found the widow at work in the shade of a huge oak tree. There was an old woodburning stove set up under the tree and smoke was issuing from the metal chimney. On it were several flat irons, all being heated. The woman was bending over an ironing board, putting finishing touches to another of his shirts.

The iron she was using had a detachable handle. When it cooled, she had simply to put it back on top of the cast iron stove to reheat, first detaching the handle which snapped into the top of a hot iron.

"Quite a setup," Barron ventured, watching her. She offered him a grin.

"Too hot to wash and iron in th' house. I set up out here in summer. It's a lot more pleasant." She placed the iron on a holder and took the bundle of black clothing Barron handed her.

"I'll have everything ready b'fore noon tomorrow," she promised, then eyed his black Stetson critically. "Take a brush to that hat and you'll look like a new man!"

The clean clothing afforded the detective a feeling of contentment that surprised him, as he walked back up the street toward the center of town. He moved to the side of the street, as a horse and buggy approached. Rita was at the reins.

Instead of passing him by, she pulled up the horse to smile at him. "You look different," she declared. "Must be Missus Stern's influence."

"Right. Where're you off to, ma'am."

She shook her head and smiled. "You don't have to be quite so polite. Everyone in town calls me Rita."

"I gather everyone in town's known you since you was a kid. That makes a difference."

"It's Rita," she insisted. "And you're Jim?"

"Right enough." She hadn't answered his question about her destination. He glanced to the West, squinting against the sun. "It's coolin' off some. Good day for a drive."

"I'm headed up to the cemetery," the woman told him, settling back against the seat. "My father's up there. I go up at least once a month."

"Oh?" From previous exposure, he had expected her to be tough and unyielding, devoid of sentiment. Then he was struck by a thought. "You know where Tim Mathis is buried?"

Surprise showed in her expression. "The other detective? I think I can find the grave," she admitted. "He's only been buried a few days." She hesitated. "Want to share a ride down the hill?"

On the buggy seat was a wicker basket covered by a cloth. She set it on the floor of the buggy and moved over, making room. Barron quickly climbed in.

"Nice horse," he observed, for lack of something better to say.

"He's from the livery stable, but I use him all the time. I don't own a horse."

Both were silent as the horse, apparently of the Morgan breed, pulled the wheeled vehicle onto what now was a dirt trail. A few minutes later, the animal took a side road without prompting by the driver.

"He seems t'know where he's goin'," Barron commented. That brought a nod and a smile from the woman.

"We seem to understand each other. And we've made this trip a good many times."

Barron glanced at the basket between his feet, curious. "You bring him a basket of treats for knowin' what you want?"

Eyes on the horse's back, Rita shook her head. "Below the cemetery, there's a nice spot down near the river." She hesitated and looked at him thoughtfully. "Sometimes I take some sandwiches and have lunch down there after I talk with my father."

"Maybe you're not the tough businesslady you pretend to be," the detective stated, staring at her with a slight frown.

Her expression tightened, the smile gone. "A woman who owns a saloon has to know when to be tough. It doesn't have to become a habit."

They were at the gate of the small cemetery that was surrounded by a wire fence. She pulled on the reins to bring the horse to a halt.

"Whoa," she ordered in a quiet tone, then nodded to the basket of food. "There're enough sandwiches in there for both of us. And a jug of cold tea."

He nodded acceptance and climbed down out of the buggy, turning to help her down. She turned to point toward a recent mound of dirt at one side of the burial ground.

"That's Tim Mathis' place," she told him quietly, then pointed in another direction. "My father's over there." She hesitated. "I like to talk to him alone."

"I understand. I'll be with Tim."

"He a friend of yours?" the woman asked.

"Sort of. We worked together."

She nodded and began to pick her way between the tombstones and wooden crosses. Jim Barron watched her for a moment. He turned, looking back over the trail they had used. There was no sign that anyone had followed them. He could not help a slight scowl, though. He didn't understand why, after her diatribe of the previous night, Rita Lansworth was suddenly so friendly. His lips curled in a wry smile. Maybe it was the clean clothes. Or it could be that knowing he was a lawman of sorts made a difference.

Shaking his head and admitting to himself that he never would understand women or their thought processes, he turned and headed for the mound of fresh earth Rita had pointed out. The final resting place for his brother was marked only by a small cross nailed together from still green, unaged lumber. Jim Barron stifled a curse of anger as he stared at the wood. Carved in the crossarm, little more that a series of scratches in the raw surface, he read:

TIMOTHY J. MATHIS
Killed by Bank Robbers
July 14, 1887

Chapter Eleven

The afternoon sun was nearing the horizon as Barron and Rita sat by the edge of the creek. It had been nearly an hour since she had spread a tablecloth from the saloon on the grass, while he tied the horse in the shade of a nearby oak tree.

Barron was gnawing on a chicken drumstick when she held out another toward him. "I told you there was enough for both of us," she said, grinning. "Want another?"

He shook his head. "I've had plenty. Cookin' like this could turn me into a fat, old man in a rush."

Rita laughed. She started to raise the drumstick to her own mouth, then changed her mind. She put it back in the basket, with a little shake of her head. She stared at him with a serious expression and a quizzical tilt of her head.

"You're a funny man, Jim Barron."

He had stripped the bone, but was still chewing. "What makes you say that?" he asked through a mouthful of chicken. Rita shook her head, puzzled.

"I don't know exactly," she admitted. "I didn't like you at first. In fact, I was quite angry when you pulled that stupid trick with your thousand-dollar bill."

"I'd come a long way," he declared with a straight face. "I was thirsty. How was it you'd just come from the bank with all those hundred dollar bills? I thought banks were places to put money, not take it out."

She laughed again. "If you weren't a bank detective, I wouldn't be telling you this. I keep some money in the office safe just in case there might be a big winner at the poker table some night. Until you came along, I've never had to break into it. That money had been resting there since before my dad died."

"Why'd you decide to run the place after he passed on?" Barron asked.

She shook her head, frowning suddenly. "I don't know, actually. I guess it was something to do while I was getting over my dad's death. Then it became a way to make a living. A habit of sorts. Most of the time, I like it. Then there are times when I hate it!"

"Did Carl Lee come out here with you?" He put the question carefully and she cast him a long look.

"Someone in town's been talking to you," she accused, but she didn't look particularly perturbed. "I went to boarding school with him back East. Some way, his folks lost all their money and pulled him out of the school. I got a note from him once saying he was in San Francisco. I didn't hear anything more for years. Then, somehow, he found out I was here. That's when he came to Silver City and I gave him a job."

Barron glanced at the sky, then back at the girl, as he started to rise. Any more questions would make her suspicious.

"It's gettin' late. We'd best be getting' back t'town." He reached down to help her to her feet. She stumbled over the basket and fell against him. Barron put his arm around her to steady her.

"Sorry." Rita's tone was embarrassed, but she forced a smile. Barron was still holding her, until she drew back, straightening her dress, not meeting his eyes.

"The pleasure is all mine."

The woman paused, looking at him as though wanting to say something. "What's the matter?" Barron asked.

One eyebrow was raised, her tone bright, as she asked, "Isn't this where the girl usually gets kissed?"

Barron looked at her for a long moment, smiling in amused fashion. He offered a shake of his head. "Afraid not. Too risky."

Rita drew back a step, staring at him with an expression approaching a glare.

"What do you mean?" she demanded.

"Some men are just as rabid about women stealin' as they are about horse thieves. I don't want your Carl Lee gunnin' for me."

Her semi-glare became a full-fledged scowl and she bent to pick up the basket and the table cloth.

"It's getting late," she declared, starting toward the buggy. Jim Barron caught up to take the basket from her hand. She refused to look at him and missed the cynical smile that forced its way to his lips.

It was nearly nine o'clock when Rita Lansworth strode into her office. She still carried the picnic basket now covered with the folded tablecloth. Barron had let her off in front of the Scarlet Lily. He had offered to drive her to her house before he took the horse and buggy back to the livery stable. The ride from the cemetery had been a silent one, and Rita had not spoken until she directed him to take her to the saloon. As he drove away, she had marched through the swinging doors without a backward look.

"Enjoy yourself?"

She did not see Carl Lee until he spoke. He was sitting in a straight-back chair in a corner. His hat on the back of his head at a jaunty angle, he seemed amused, but there was a disturbed expression in his eyes. He was cold sober.

Rita whirled to face him, taking a step to stare down at him. Her face suddenly reflected the anger she had been holding back. "Why aren't you out there doing what you're paid to do?" she demanded, dropping the picnic basket on the floor.

Carl Lee rose slowly from the chair, taking off his hat. He dropped it on the chair before he spoke. "I've been waiting to see you. There are a couple of things I think we ought to get straightened out."

He waited an instant to judge her reaction, then continued. "I heard about you driving out of town this afternoon with that gun hand."

"Jim Barron? He's a bank detective, Carl, not a gun hand!" Her tone was clipped and precise. "His is a more honest profession than yours! Or mine!"

Lee shook his head, his attitude dogged. "I don't like the way he's hanging around you, Rita. I don't want to see you get hurt!"

She flared. "Are you trying to tell me who I can and can't talk to?"

Carl Lee stared at her for a long moment, then seemed to reach a decision. He heaved a deep sigh, starting to speak slowly.

"No, Rita. I'm only remembering the times when a girl used to ask me to go on picnics with here. Remember?"

Some of Rita's anger seemed to fade as she walked around her desk and sat down in her chair. "I remember, Carl, but that was a long time ago. And you've changed. What happened to you in those years after you left school?"

Lee felt he suddenly had gained acceptance and bent

to put his hands on her desk to look at her. He shook his head. "I haven't changed, Rita." He hesitated, then plunged on. "And there's something I'd better tell you about Jim Barron."

He straightened and reached to his inside coat pocket to bring out a folded rectangle of paper. He unfolded it slowly and handed it to the woman, waiting to see her reaction. He seemed satisfied, when she suddenly stiffened at what she saw.

"Where'd you get this?" she demanded. It was the old poster offering the $1,000 reward for Jim Barron.

"Where I got it isn't important," he stated. "And I didn't want you to learn about it this way, Rita. I didn't want to be the one to tell you."

She shook her head, looking down once more at the soiled poster. "I don't understand. He's a detective. A bank detective."

He reached down to pick up the poster, folding it and returning it to his pocket, as he spoke. "Perhaps he only says that's what he is."

Rita's features had settled into acceptance. The decision made her look older and less attractive. "Does the sheriff know about this?" she asked.

"He's been in Albuquerque on county business for more than a week. He got back today."

"Does he know?" Rita's tone was insistent. Carl Lee nodded.

"He knows. I talked with him this afternoon after I woke up. He's doing some checking and he doesn't want anything said about this to anyone. Understand?" Lee's voice was suddenly urgent.

"What do you mean?"

"The sheriff thinks Barron may have had something to do with the bank robbery. He may even have been the lookout who shot that man in the back!"

"But what's going to happen?"

"The sheriff's keeping a close eye on Barron. Giving him a chance to use up all his rope before the hanging."

Rita shook her head, looking away. "I don't understand it, Carl. Jim Barron does not seem like a robber and a killer."

Carl Lee could not keep a cynical note out of his tone. He was on a roll and took advantage of it. "Folks that knew him said Jesse James didn't either." He paused, tone suddenly urgent. "Just remember. Don't say anything to anyone."

Rita nodded and rose from her chair as Lee picked up his hat. "I'll walk you home," he offered. She offered a silent nod, opened the door and led the way into the barroom.

Jim Barron, standing at the bar, watched as they passed through the swinging doors into the night. Charlie Reese, wiping glasses behind the bar, watched them, too. Several card players also followed the pair with their eyes until they disappeared beyond the doors.

"Make a right nice lookin' couple, don't you think?"

"Yeah. Just lovely." Barron had difficulty keeping the sarcasm out of his tone.

Charlie glanced at Barron, puzzled by his words. He shrugged them off, however, warming to his subject.

"Carl's maybe a little on th' wild side from time t'time, but he wouldn't be any kinda gambler if he wasn't. Rita might be able t'straighten him out, if she'd just break down and marry him!"

Barron glanced at the bartender, then pushed away from the bar, stalking across the floor, through the doors and into the night. The bartender stared after him for a moment, brow wrinkled. Then, with a shrug, he returned to his labors.

Chapter Twelve

It was after nine o'clock when Rita Lansworth came into the Scarlet Lily, pausing to glance about. Except for Charlie Reese, who was taking the chairs off the tables and arranging them for coming business, there was no one present but the swamper. The floor was freshly mopped, still damp.

"Good morning, Charlie," she called from the spot near the door where she had paused. "Have you seen Carl this morning?

Reese paused to offer her a shake of his head. "No ma'am. He ain't been in yet."

Rita nodded, as though understanding there might be a reason for Lee's absence, then turned to look over the top of the swinging doors. On the opposite side of the street, Jim Barron and Lem Turner were walking together, involved in deep conversation. The banker seemed to be protesting something the detective had said. Rita watched and was surprised when the two turned into the sheriff's office. Carl Lee had said he told the sheriff about the price on Barron's head.

Puzzled, she turned from the door and headed toward her office, glancing at Reese as she passed. "Could I have some black coffee, Charlie?"

"Right away, ma'am. I'll bring it in." He removed the last chair from atop a table and put it in place before he headed for the back room where stores were kept and coffee brewed. He wondered what was bothering Rita. The whole town knew about her buggy ride with Jim Barron, of course. That could have something to do with it.

At the jail, introductions had been made and Sheriff Wyatt Ord waved the two men to chairs. He looked at Barron with a grim smile. "Good thing you stopped in, Barron. I was about t'come lookin' for you."

"Oh?" Barron didn't try to hide his surprise.

"A young feller come in here yesterday with a wanted poster on you. Told me he expected to collect th' reward."

"Carl Lee?" Barron asked, eyes narrowing. The sheriff nodded.

"Somethin' didn't sound right about what he was tellin', so I wired th' warden at Fort Madison prison. His answer back said you'd served your time and were gone. Also said you'd been a model prisoner.

"Then I wired Alan Jensen in Kay Cee to find out whether you really are a Jensen agent. Jensen's outa town, but a young man I talked with said you're down here tryin' to learn who killed your brother." The sheriff glanced at Lem Turner. "You didn't know him and Tim Mathis were brothers, did you?" The question caused Turner to stare at Barron, frowning.

"Half-brothers," Barron corrected, "but we always were pretty close."

Well, I better tell young Lee you're not wanted so he don't try t'kill you for th' bounty," the sheriff said. This caused Barron to shake his head, scowling.

"No! Don't do that!" he ordered. "I'm in with th' gang, b'cause they think I'm wanted. This'll all be over in a day or so. Meantime, I'll watch out for Carl Lee!"

"You sure that's what you want?" the sheriff asked carefully. "Bounty hunters don't usually give a man a fair play."

"I can handle it," Barron announced grimly. He was wondering how Lee had come into possession of the reward poster. It had been in Jake Gibson's hands the last he had seen of it.

The sheriff's nod was reluctant. "Well, don't you go shootin' him, unless you got witnesses that he drew first. Up till th' bank robbery, I had a nice, quiet town here. I'd like t'keep it that way. Any idea who's involved in this?"

Barron hesitated, then nodded. "Jake Gibson's in it

up to his neck, but he ain't runnin' the operation. Doesn't have the brains for it. What do you know about him?"

The sheriff frowned for a moment, collecting his thoughts before replying. "He's been around here a coupla months. Heads up three or four others claimin' they're workin' a mine back in th' hills.

"They ever come into town with any ore?" Barron wanted to know. The sheriff shook his head.

"Not that I've heard about. Up where they say they're workin', others've tried and didn't find silver."

Lem Turner had not uttered a word after the initial introductions. He sat on the edge of his chair, gripping the wooden arms nervously. Suddenly, he interrupted. "The money I've borrowed is coming in on the stage first thing tomorrow, but even the driver doesn't know it. I'll need lots of protection around the bank after that. If I lose this shipment, the bank's busted. So're a lot of people around here!"

"Th' smart thing'd be for you to hire a coupla full-time security guards," the sheriff offered, settling back in his chair to eye the banker. "Me or my deputies can't camp over there forever, you know."

"I don't think that'll be necessary," Barron put in. "I'll know more later today, but I think they plan on hittin' th' bank tomorrow afternoon." He rose from his chair suddenly. "In fact, I oughta be gettin' out there to sit in on th' plannin'!"

He turned toward the door and the banker rose to

follow him. "Thanks, sheriff," Barron said over his shoulder. "I'll be in touch."

On the sidewalk outside, Barron nodded at the banker. "I have to get a move on."

"I hope we can wrap this whole thing up once and for all," Lem Turner fretted. He shook Barron's hand and turned to plod up the street. Across the way, Rita Lansworth had just come out of the saloon and paused to watch the two of them. She had the leather folder in her hand in which she took each day's receipts to the bank. Barron saw her, but made no gesture to let her know it. Instead, he hurried toward the livery stable.

"Got your horse saddled and ready, just like you ordered," the liveryman reported, as Barron entered the barn. "Been doin' it every day, but he's getting' fat, just standin' in th' stall."

"Well, maybe I can work some of it off him," Barron said. "I'm gonna ride up into th' hills a bit. Maybe be gone most of th' day."

Carl Lee was currying his own mount in one of the stalls and overheard the exchange. Bending low so Barron wouldn't see him, he listened as the detective led his mount out to bridle him, then tightened the cinch. As Barron rode out of the barn, Lee edged out of the stall and grabbed his own saddle off a rack. Hurriedly, he began to saddle his gray mare. He was certain Barron was headed for the gang's headquarters at the worked-out mine. The trail Jake Gibson had followed to take him up there had been long, difficult and even torturous, but he later had found another route that was faster and shorter. He assumed this was an escape route the gang would use if ever attacked. Barron would have to follow the trail he knew.

His horse ready, Carl Lee went to the manger in the stall and dug under the old hay and straw. Out of it came a single-shot .50 caliber Sharps buffalo rifle. He jammed the rifle into the scabbard already attached to the saddle and mounted, riding out of the barn with a wave at the stable operator who stood near the entrance.

Jim Barron had no difficulty retracing the route he had followed in the dark until he reached the plateau where the outlaw, Sid, had left him. After that, it became a tracking problem. Luckily, there had been no rain to wash out the tracks, but some of them had been swept away by the winds. Several times he had to circle to pick tracks farther along. He also had to dodge the cacti that seemed to seek him out. He wished he had bought a pair of chaps for this kind of country.

Suddenly there was a rifle shot that clipped a large cactus a foot in front of the gelding's nose. Barron bailed off the horse, grabbing his Winchester carbine from its scabbard in the same move.

Slapping the horse on the rump, he ran for a collection of boulders twenty yards away, making cover as another heavy-caliber bullet bounced off the rock in his wake.

Behind the cover he had selected, Carl Lee was cursing the .50 caliber Sharps rifle. He had never fired it before and the first shot had recoiled heavily against his shoulder. On the second shot he had flinched, reacting against the expected pain and, at the same time, throwing the shot wide. He had won the rifle in a poker game with a few rounds of ammunition. Carefully, he ejected the empty brass case, loaded another big round into the chamber and closed the action. Ready once more, he looked carefully over the top of the rock behind which he had been waiting for Barron to appear.

Barron's shot struck the boulder next to his face, peeling off a sharp splinter of rock that slashed across Lee's cheek. It destroyed his aim, as he fired the Sharps. Head lowered, he pressed his hand to his cheek, drawing it back to see the blood the sliver had started running. Propping up the rifle to keep it out of the dirt, he pulled a handkerchief from his pocket and clamped it to the cut. Frightened, he grabbed the rifle and half crawled, scuttling down the hill to where his horse was tied.

Listening and waiting, Barron heard the click of steel shoes on rock as the bushwhacker departed. Rifle still in hand and using caution, he dodged toward the spot where the rifleman had waited.

Behind the rock Lee had used for cover, he found

the empty Sharps cases, prints of boots and a couple of flecks of blood on the sand. Pocketing the expended brass, he wondered how badly the other man was hit. Looking out across the plateau, there was no sign of a rider. Probably sticking to the canyons, Barron told himself.

Walking back to where his horse was grazing on the sparse shrubbery, Barron shoved the Model 94 into the scabbard and swung into the saddle, taking up the trail again. It was slow going and more than another hour passed before he came in sight of the abandoned mine and the shack Gibson's gang was using as a headquarters.

As he rode down the hill toward the weathered structure, he saw no sign of a lookout, but he was certain there was one. Four horses were saddled and tied to a makeshift hitch rack in front of the cabin. Without hesitation, he rode up to the railing, swung down and tied his own horse. He glanced about, then walked to the door and pounded on it.

"It's Barron," he called at the same time. "Let me in."

"Door's open," came the answer.

Barron entered, eyes unaccustomed to the dimness. Blinking, he noted that one of the men was asleep in one of the bunks. Jake Gibson was seated behind the rickety table and Mitch was standing at his elbow. It appeared they had been studying a paper spread on the table before them.

"What're you doin' here?" Gibson wanted to know, tone verging on a snarl.

"I figured you'd want to know what's happening, so I rode up." Barron tried to keep his tone conversational, noting that Mitch had his right hand, fingers splayed, close to his holster.

"People're waitin' things out," Barron announced. "They're waitin' to see what happens, but they're nervous. I talked Turner into bringing in a batch of fresh money from another bank. Twenty-five thousand."

"It's comin' in on th' mornin' stage?" Gibson asked. Barron nodded.

"We can hit th' bank when they first open in th' mornin'," Barron announced. "It should be simple."

His next question was phrased to sound innocent. "We'd best do some plannin'. Who stayed with th' horses on that last job?"

"I did, Mister Barron." It was Mitch who snarled an answer, his body tense and ready to draw. "Pretty smart, posin' as a badman so we'd take you in."

Barron said nothing. Instead, he took a step away from the table, hand hovering over his own sixgun, as he returned Mitch's stare.

"Draw, Barron, and Sid'll kill you." Gibson was looking past Barron's shoulder to where Sid stood with a rifle leveled at the detective. Barron slowly turned his head to take in the situation, then elevated his hands to shoulder height. With a quick step, Mitch stepped in to jerk the sixgun from his holster. Barron seemed not to care as he stared now at Gibson, eyes narrowed.

"One of you was listenin' outside Lem Taylor's window th' other night," he accused. "Which one tried t'bushwhack me on th' trail a bit ago?"

Gibson rose from behind the table, grinning. He shook his head. "No more of your tricks, Barron. We got a few of our own. While your people're expectin' us to hit th' bank, we'll be takin' th' money off that stagecoach."

Barron offered an amiable nod, smiling at Gibson. "Smart," he conceded. "Who thought that up?"

"What'cha mean?" Gibson's question was openly belligerent, though marked with surprise. Barron shook his head.

"You ain't smart enough t'ramrod this sort of business, Jake. And you ain't half bright enough to think out a switch like this!"

Enraged by the insult in Barron's tone, Gibson stepped forward to smash a fist into his face. Barron was driven backward a step or so, but dropped his hands, starting to charge Gibson. Sid stepped forward, raised the rifle and crashed the butt into the back of Barron's skull.

As the detective fell loosely to the floor, Gibson stepped forward to kick him viciously in the ribs. Mitch lowered the muzzle of his sixgun and pulled back the hammer, ready to fire.

"Not now!" Gibson ordered. "You'll get your chance, when we need a corpse that's fresh!"

Chapter Thirteen

Carl Lee was mopping the cut on his cheek with a white silk handkerchief as he came through the bat-wing doors of the Scarlet Lily. Charlie Reese, who had been straightening up behind the bar, stared at him with a frown. The cut was still seeping blood and was obvious, but the bartender didn't mention it. Nor did he say anything about the trail dust that had settled on Lee's black suit.

"Where've you been?" he demanded. "Miss Rita's been askin' for you."

Lee ignored the question, coming to lean on the bar, again holding the handkerchief to the damaged cheek. "Give me a drink!"

Reese stared at him for a long moment, then offered a slight shrug, bringing a shot glass from beneath the bar and turning to grab a bottle off the back bar. He poured the whiskey, then watched as Carl Lee grabbed the glass and downed it in a single gulp.

"Carl, where have you been?" Rita was standing in the door of her office, her scowl more an expression of worry than anger. As the gambler turned toward her, he lowered the handkerchief and she saw the ragged cut on his face. "What happened to your face?"

Carl offered a shake of his head, looking down at the blood on the square of silk rather than returning her gaze.

"Cut myself with my razor a bit ago. Shaky, I reckon."

"Come on back here. We need to talk about some things!" Her voice was suddenly stern, and Carl Lee shook his head once more, glancing at the bartender. Rita had retreated into her office.

"Why can't she just leave me be?" he asked fretfully. Charlie Reese shook his head, still frowning, but there was a comforting note in his tone.

"She's worried about you, I reckon. She knows you've been drinkin' too much. Look at you. You're nervous as an alley cat in a dog house!"

Lee cast the bartender a look of disgust, then moved toward the office doorway. Reese picked up the empty shot glass, eyed it with what could be interpreted as speculation and slid it under the bar.

Rita had left the office door open, and as Lee entered, she turned from where she had been standing looking out into the alley through a curtained window. "Shut the door," she ordered. The gambler did as told, then shuffled to a chair in the corner, dropping into it and covering his eyes with his hands for a moment. Rita Lansworth waited, expecting him to speak. Finally, she made the plunge.

"I asked you a minute ago where you've been."

Lee looked up, matching her frown with one of his own. "I haven't been feeling well. I took a nap, then I shaved and came here. What's this all about?"

"I went over to the hotel and looked in your room, Carl. You weren't there. And the desk clerk said he saw you ride out of town earlier." He moved past her desk to stare down at him. "And look at your clothes. They're filthy. Are you mixed up in something?"

Carl Lee rose from the chair to stare at her. As a poker player, he long ago had learned to control his facial expressions. When he spoke, his tone was one of indignation. "What do you mean? What're you trying to say?"

The woman heaved a sigh, looking away for a moment. When her eyes came back to Carl, the anger was gone. There was only an expression that seemed to combine disappointment and sadness.

"There's something you should know, Carl." She shook her head, the frowning starting to return to her face. "I probably should have told you a long time ago that I know."

Carl Lee's expression went from indignation to one

that was guarded. "Know what?" he demanded, tone suddenly brusque.

"Those two years of your life that you've never talked about, Carl. I know you were in California, just as you claimed." She hesitated for a moment, biting her lower lip before going on. She knew admitting her knowledge was going to be painful.

"I know you were in prison," she said slowly in a flat monotone, a statement of fact. Carl Lee stiffened as he heard the words. He frowned, searching her face, wanting to see something there he had missed. Then he suddenly relaxed, a weight off his shoulders.

"But if you knew all this, why would you. . . ."

She interrupted, shaking her head. "I wanted you to straighten out your life by yourself, Carl. I thought you could do it. Become a man. An honest man. I've been waiting for that to happen. That's the reason I haven't married you." Her tone was sympathetic and she paused for a moment, searching his face for answers. "What kind of trouble are you in?"

Carl Lee suddenly rebelled. Whether he was rebelling against this woman, himself or just the world, he didn't know. "I'm not in any trouble," he snarled. "And I don't need your sympathy! I don't want you feeling sorry for me!"

Rita reached out to place a comforting hand on his shoulder. "That isn't it at all, Carl." She said it quietly, but the sadness was still reflected in her tone. The gambler reached up to take her hand, cupping it between both of his own.

"Then let's get out of here, Rita." His tone was suddenly excited, as though he was within sight of a goal he had sought for so long. "Charlie would buy the place on time. We could get married in Las Cruces or Deming and keep right on going."

The woman stared at him strangely, then withdrew her hand. Carl seemed not to notice the sudden rebuff. He was staring at her, grinning.

"I'll be coming into some money in a day or two, Rita. Lots of it! We can do it then. Just leave!"

Carl Lee realized suddenly he had said too much. He stopped talking, staring at her as though awaiting her decision. His sudden scowl became an expression of wistful desire, as he realized he had struck a nerve.

"Where are you going to get a lot of money? You are in trouble," Rita charged angrily. "You want to run and you're selfish enough to want me to run with you."

Carl Lee reached out as though to take her by the shoulder, but Rita stepped back, shaking her head. "You'd better leave, Carl. I don't know what to think about you now."

He offered a sigh, staring at the floor and shaking his head. His tone was dogged as he mumbled. "I'm not in trouble, Rita." But he turned and moved to the door, shutting it behind him as he edged into the saloon.

Rita Lansworth moved to her desk and dropped into the padded chair that had belonged to her father. It had become hers along with all of the responsibility of running the Scarlet Lily and she found it comforting. Just sitting there, she often felt as though she was communicating with her father. This feeling usually came about when she faced a serious problem or was overly tired. She expected the same feeling of emotional comfort now, but it didn't come.

The woman heaved a sigh and dropped her head to rest it on her folded arms. Most of the time, running the saloon was not that difficult. The occasional problems, she had found, were usually caused by the fact that she was a woman and received no respect from men, when it came to business. They didn't understand how she could make a go of what had always been a man's business, and some of them even resented her successes.

Carl Lee had been a definite help, for he had run an honest poker game, as she insisted. He had told her he didn't know how to cheat—not well, at least—and she had accepted that. Now she wondered.

Charlie Reese was also a find. She had hired him not long after her father had died and she had taken over. The bartenders who had worked for her father did not want to have the signals called by a woman and had drifted on. She was tending bar herself until the day Reese had walked in the door and asked for a job. He took care of the day bar, while two other bartenders switched off on night duty. Charlie was popular with the customers and even the businessmen of the town seemed to respect him.

Sitting there, her head on her folded arms, Rita Lansworth realized she was confused. She had been confused for a long time, but had not allowed it to gain a foothold in her subconscious. She did not want to continue operating the Scarlet Lily. Like other women, she wanted a home and children, but none of the men with whom she came in contact stood up to her ideals. For the most part, they were cowboys, miners, middle-aged businessmen. Most of them had wives and kids of their own.

And adding to her confusion now was Jim Barron. He had come in off the street and aroused her anger by trying to cash that $1,000 bill for a ten-cent beer! She wondered now whether it was a ploy to get her attention. She'd have to ask him about it sometime. He was honest enough to tell her, she thought.

She smiled through what had threatened to be tears only moments before. She could never sell the Scarlet Lily and leave town with Carl Lee. She had always known he would ask eventually and she had known she would have to refuse. They had been friends in childhood, of course, and Lee had been an asset in the business, until now.

Jim Barron was quite another thing. She had learned during their picnic beside the stream that he could be thoughtful and introspective. There were moments when he dropped his stone-faced expression to offer a laugh. When she had flirted and suggested he should kiss her, she had marveled at the way he had handled it. Most of the men she knew would have been all over her!

Poised there behind her desk, she wondered what kind of trouble it was that Carl Lee had brought upon himself. And she wondered whether it had anything to do with Jim Barron's mission to find the bank robbers.

In the bar, Carl Lee had downed another shot of raw whiskey and was rapping on the bar with the shot glass. Charlie Reese glanced at him and shook his head.

"You've had enough, Carl," he intoned. "You'd best get t'your room and clean up so you can earn your keep here t'night."

"I always earn my keep," the gambler half snarled, but he turned the shot glass loose and moved uncertainly toward the swinging doors.

"You'd best have the doc look at that cut, too," Reese called after him. "Looks like it's deep enough t'leave a scar. He may wanta take some stitches!"

But Carl Lee was already through the doors and clumping down the board sidewalk as Lem Turner looked in, then entered. He glanced over his shoulder with a frown before he walked up to the bar.

"What happened to Carl's face?" he wanted to know. The bartender shook his head. "Somethin' he don't wanta talk about. Coffee's hot. I'll get you a cup."

The banker shook his head, frowning suddenly. "I don't have time, Charlie. I'm looking for Jim Barron. Have you seen him?

"No. Not this morning. What's up with him?"

"I just got a telegram from Alan Jensen, his boss. Alan's been in Deming and is coming in on the afternoon stage. He wants to hold a meeting with Barron and myself." Turner shook his head. "He's had four banks in this area robbed in less than two months. I really think he's down here in person trying to patch fences with his clients, but who knows?"

"Your bank open this morning?" the bartender asked thoughtfully. "Can I come and get my money?"

"If you really want to close out your account, it'd be better to wait until this afternoon," the banker suggested. "Maybe about three o'clock. I wish you wouldn't do it though. We'll go on being a bank."

He turned toward the door, shaking his head. "Right now, I have to find Barron!"

Chapter Fourteen

Rita came out of her office, pausing thoughtfully to look around the big room. It was almost as though she was wondering how she came to be there. Finally, her eyes settled on Charlie Reese, who had the local weekly newspaper spread out on the bar.

"Where did Carl go, Charlie?" Her question caused the bartender to look up from his reading.

"I told him t'go get cleaned up for work, but t'see Doc Dougherty b'fore he comes in. That cut looks like it needs a coupla stitches."

Rita shook her head. "I don't know what it is with him. The past couple of months, he's seemed like a different man."

"Yeah, I've noticed some of that," the bartender

agreed. "Lem Turner was in, too. He was lookin' for Jim Barron."

The woman turned worried eyes upon him. "More trouble?"

"I don't think so. He said th' head of that detective agency Barron works for's on his way into town. He wants a meet with Barron and Lem, I guess."

"I haven't seen Jim, either," Rita mused, wondering where he might be. She had been hoping he would come have morning coffee with her.

Jim Barron had been conscious for what he guessed to be more than an hour. It was hot in the cabin and he had regained his senses, plus a splitting headache, only to find his hands tied behind his back with what he took to be strips of rawhide. During all the time that had passed since he had opened his eyes, he had been working on his bindings.

Rawhide shrinks as it dries. If these strips had been wet when he was bound, they probably would have cut off the circulation, Barron realized. But with no air stirring and the sun pounding down on the roof, it had to be more than a hundred degrees in the shack. He was perspiring profusely, and as a result of the blow he had taken, felt as though his head had been divided with a meat cleaver. If the leather absorbed enough of the sweat from his arms and wrists, he should be able to stretch the wet thongs enough to escape.

Upon regaining consciousness, he had lain there for several minutes, keeping his eyes closed until he was certain he was alone. Then he sat up to look around for some tool he could use to cut the leather strips. He saw nothing. Working the bonds as he had, though, he was certain they were a bit looser.

And as he struggled for release, his mind kept reviewing what had happened and how he had come to be in this situation. It was not quite the way he had planned things. He knew Jake Gibson was not the one running the gang. He simply took orders and supplied the gun hands for whatever job someone else had researched and laid out. That much was obvious, Barron realized, but it put him no closer to learning the identity of the real ramrod of the outfit, the person responsible for Tim's death.

Barron still wore his gun belt, but had no idea where his sixgun might be. It was nowhere in the room that he could see. Also, he saw no sign of his black Stetson. Had one of the outlaws decided it was better headwear than his own? More important, why was he still alive? Why had he been tied up instead of simply being shot in the head and dropped into a nearby canyon? A lot of what was happening just didn't make sense.

And amid all of this, Barron's thoughts also drifted to Rita Lansworth and Carl Lee. He had no doubt that the man who had attempted to bushwack him was the gambler. Was he after the $1,000 reward, not aware that it had been rescinded long ago? Or was it jealousy over the woman?

Much as he disliked even having the thought enter his head, Barron also wondered whether Rita could be the one giving the orders to the gang, with Lee as the messenger. Had her sudden friendliness been strictly for the purposes of pumping him for information? Barron realized his brain was still somewhat befuddled from the earlier blow, but found he was feeling ashamed at even allowing such a question to enter his mind.

The feeling of guilt and revulsion may have given his efforts in seeking freedom a little added strength, for he felt a knot slip in the rawhide bindings. An instant later, he was able to remove his right hand from the thong's hold and bring it around his body to look at. Then he checked the other hand, taking time to flex his cramped fingers slowly, gritting his teeth against the pain.

Both wrists were raw and bloody, and he realized it was blood as much as perspiration that had softened the rawhide. He was on the point of rising when he heard the crunch of boots on the rock outside the cabin. He dropped back to the floor, grabbing the rawhide strips before putting his hands behind his back. Working with clumsy fingers, he sought to encircle his wrists with the rawhide thongs.

His back was toward the door, but he heard it open and close, then steps approached him across the loose board floor. A boot toe was inserted beneath his rib cage and used to jostled him.

"Come on, Barron. I know you're awake. Quit fakin'," the voice ordered. It sounded like Sid, who seemed to be the least competent of the gang. It would be natural to leave him on guard duty. But, again, he was back to the question of why a guard was needed and he wasn't dead.

"Maybe this'll wake you up," the guard muttered and Barron slitted his eyes just enough to see that the rifle barrel was being lowered toward his cheek. The end of the barrel carried a front sight that must have been battered against rocks at some time in its history. The edge of the sight was ragged and sharp along its upper edge.

The sight was pressed against his cheek and the guard pulled it upward with a sudden motion that slashed the skin. Without moving, Barron felt a sudden gush of blood channeling down his cheek to drip on the floor. He wondered if he had flinched at the pain. He must have, he realized, when he heard Sid's next words.

"Come on, Barron, get up b'fore I make that face of yours look like five pounds of rotten liver!"

Again, Barron didn't move. After a moment, he heard an exasperated sigh and the contact of heels with the floor, as Sid turned away. In spite of the crashing headache that made him doubt his own capabilities, Barron rolled quickly to his knees. As the rifleman, startled by the sound behind him, started to turn, the detective crashed into his lower legs, wrapping both arms around them. There was satisfaction in hearing the rifle clatter on the boards as it was thrown from Sid's grasp. Part of the outlaw's weight fell on him, but Barron ignored the pain along his spine.

Both men were now on the floor, kicking and clawing for advantage. Barron was aware that he had heard the thump caused by Sid's sixgun falling from its holster. The outlaw managed to roll free and grabbed for the rifle he had dropped. On his knees, he brought the muzzle up, swinging toward Barron.

The detective, though, now had Sid's sixgun in his own grasp. As the rifle barrel swung to center on his chest, he thumbed back the hammer of the single action Colt and fired a round into the outlaw's throat at a range of no more than three feet. Sid coughed and the rifle slid from his hands. Barron backed away and rose to his feet. He started to jam Sid's sixgun into his own holster, then he paused to check the caliber. It was .44–40, the same as his own. He jammed the piece into his holster and looked around for his hat, but there was no sign of it.

Sid's sweat-stained headwear lay in a corner and Barron picked it up, jamming it on his own head. It was too large, but there was a latigo tie that he pulled up under his chin to hold the crushed piece of felt in place.

When he looked around, he saw that Sid was dead, his eyes open and staring with an expression of terror. Acting with what he considered misplaced pity, Jim Barron pulled a colorful Mexican-made blanket from one of the unmade bunks and spread it over the body. Someone else would have to worry about the niceties of death.

At the door, Barron turned back and picked up the rifle the outlaw had been carrying. It was a single-shot Remington Baby Carbine that was chambered for the .44 Winchester cartridge. He looked about the cabin, checking several shelves for the proper ammunition, but saw none. Then he thought of the late outlaw's saddlebags. They weren't in the shack, either, but when he stepped outside, still carrying the single-shot lead slinger, he found the horse, saddled and ready, tied to the hitchrail. To Barron's surprise, his own horse was missing. First his hat and sixgun. Now his horse. He was bothered, growing increasingly aware that he and his belongings were being used in some way that called for Gibson and the others to keep him alive a while longer.

He closed the door to keep the coyotes and other scavengers from getting to the corpse, then went to Sid's horse, a thin, nondescript animal that needed about fifty pounds more meat on him to put him in good shape. Searching the saddlebags, Baron found another sixgun—not his own—and almost full boxes of ammo for both the handgun and the rifle. From the way the front sight had been banged about—including on his own cheek—he didn't have much faith in the rifle, but it had to be better than none at all. He stuffed it into the scabbard attached to the saddle, then mounted.

When he reached for his gold watch, he found it missing. Glancing at the sun, he read it as standing at somewhere around three o'clock. Maybe a bit less. He knew where he had to go and spurred the undernourished horse down the trail without a backward glance.

Chapter Fifteen

Alan Jensen had been surprised to find that he was the only passenger on the stagecoach from Deming to Silver City. Then, when he learned they were carrying $25,000 bound for Lem Turner's Cattleman's Savings Bank, he wondered whether word had gotten out and Deming residents who might otherwise have traveled were afraid of being in the middle of a holdup.

That possibility had occupied his thoughts over most of the trip, interspersed with his own problems of keeping his business together. There had been four bank robberies right in this same area of New Mexico all within a few months. All of the banks were clients of the Jensen Detective Agency and, to this point, none of the money had been recovered or the bandits caught.

Tim Mathis had been sent to New Mexico to run down the outlaws and had indicated by telegram that he was finally on the track of the band when he had been killed. Ironically, Jensen mused, it had been during the holdup of the Silver City bank.

In what he now recognized as a fit of anger and frustration, he had hired Jim Barron to identify and bring in the bank bandits. But since his arrival in Silver City, Barron had not contacted him once, and that worried him. Admittedly, it was not unlike the way Barron had always worked before he went to prison, but in those days, the Jensen Detective Agency had been growing and its agents—primarily Barron—had been catching bank bandits. He had been allowed to march to the beat of his own drum as long as he showed results.

Now, though, things were different, Jensen fretted. He didn't know what Barron was doing. He had even sent a telegram to Lem Turner, seeking assurances that Barron was on the job, but that had not been answered. Barron had always tended to ignore the telegraph system, voicing the belief that there were too many operators along the way who could decipher a message and perhaps pass it to the wrong people. This excuse had made sense of a sort, but did nothing to calm Alan Jensen's current misgivings.

From the Deming banker, he had learned that the money being sent as a loan to Lem Turner was all in gold. It was in the strongbox chained to the seat between the driver and the shotgun guard and seemed safe enough. Jensen had long ago tired of the scenery visible through the open windows on each side of the coach, but he kept watching, alternating his gaze from one window to the other, looking for possible areas of ambush.

In spite of his discomfort and misgivings about recent history, he also felt an almost forgotten thrill of excitement building somewhere within. He had started the agency more than twenty years ago and had been its first and—for several years—only agent. Operating alone, he had been successful in clearing up several robberies and recovering most of the loot. Some of these successes had come about more by luck than good detective work, he had admitted to himself during moments of self-evaluation, but never to anyone else. That had gotten him a good play across the country in the newspapers, and other banks had come looking for his protection. He had made numerous trips about the country, calling on client banks, but this was the first time in years that he had been aboard a coach that he knew was carrying a big sum of money. He couldn't help a slight smile. This was sort of like old times.

As nearly as he could determine, Jim Barron had gotten nowhere in his investigations of the Silver City robbery. This might be the time to lay him off and bring in another investigator. Maybe even take over the investigation himself. He knew he could not keep

Barron on the payroll once this matter was settled. No matter what the man learned or how good he was, Jensen knew it simply was not good business to have an ex-convict working for him.

The land along the early part of the trail was reasonably level, and the driver of the coach had held the team at a steady, space-covering trot for a good portion of the trip. As they entered the forest area below Silver City, the pace slowed. He had tried to sleep earlier in the day, but it hadn't worked. Jensen was nervous, seeing every clump of tall evergreens as a potential ambush site. In addition, he finally admitted to himself that he was worried about Jim Barron and what his reactions might be when he was fired. Barron, he knew, tended to be a violent man, and he had no idea of what those years in prison had done to him.

Barron's father had died during a diphtheria epidemic and Mary, his mother, still a young woman, had remarried Clarence Mathis, a Missouri farmer. In the first year of their marriage, Tim had been born. Barron was 5 at the time. Both adults had died in a tornado that hit the farm when Barron was 15. Thus, it had been pretty much up to Barron to take care of his younger half-brother.

Jim Barron had told Jensen nothing of their early life, but Tim talked of it from time to time after his half-brother went to prison. Barron had managed to get through nine years of school, then had quit to break horses and do ranch labor like building fences and reshingling barns, chores most working cowboys hated. He had plodded along at those and other unpleasant jobs so Tim could finish high school.

Jim Barron had captured a couple of outlaws down in Texas when barely out of his teens and had made quite a splash in the newspapers. That was how Jensen had heard of him and, after interviewing him, had hired him as an apprentice investigator. In less than a year, Barron had been handling his own cases and, in most instances, bringing them to satisfactory conclusions. Several years later, he had talked the agency owner into hiring Tim, who had done his apprenticeship under his older brother. Barron had taught him everything he knew.

Their temperaments were a mile apart, Jensen mused as the coach rumbled along. Jim had been the type who trusted no one and was slow to turn his back on those he did. Tim, on the other hand, might well have been too trusting, thinking well of his fellow man, until he learned otherwise. With Jim's attitude, Jensen thought, you never knew what could happen. For a moment, he found himself wondering whether he was a little bit afraid of Jim Barron.

As the coach hit a rut and swayed from side to side, Jensen removed his derby and laid it on the seat beside him. He used a red bandana to wipe the dust and perspiration from his face. He was looking forward to reaching Silver City, where he could get a bath and a shave.

On a low ridge flanking the trail, hidden by the forest growth, Gibson, Troy Mitchell and another rider called Grits drew rein and watched the coach pass below. Gibson shook his head in anger.

"He's ahead of schedule. I wanted t'ambush him." He looked at the other two. "Get down there and get that coach stopped!"

Mitch and Grits pulled bandanas up to cover their faces. Mitch was wearing Jim Barron's black Stetson, had the detective's sixgun in his holster and was astride the detective's black gelding. Without a word from Gibson, the two spurred their horses down the low hill at an angle toward the stagecoach. In a few moments, they were lost in the dust thrown up by the hooves and the coach horses and the fast turning wheels.

The driver and and the shotgun guard were unaware they had company until Mitch suddenly rode up beside the guard and shot him. The guard slumped, but tried to raise his scattergun. Mitch shot him again, this time in the head, and he tumbled off the seat to sprawl in the road.

The driver tried to whip up the horses, but Grits had galloped ahead and grabbed one of the lead team by the bridle, causing it to slow. Alan Jensen heard the shots. As the coach was brought to a halt, he looked out and saw the man holding the team. His satchel was at his feet and he bent to open it and pull forth a long-barreled Colt Peacemaker.

Cocking the gun, he leaned far enough out the window to see that the masked rider who had stopped the horses was riding back toward the coach. As Jensen took aim, a revolver barrel slashed down across his wrist. The blow sent the sixgun spinning from his grip and he sat staring at the wrist, which appeared to be broken.

"Out of th' coach," Jake Gibson ordered. He was standing at the side of the coach, his gun in one hand, holding his horse with the other. He too was masked. As Alan Jensen slowly dismounted from the coach, gripping his injured wrist, Gibson cast a quick glance at Mitch. The latter had dismounted and had Barron's sixgun angled upward at the driver.

"Throw that strongbox down here," Mitch ordered. The driver, hands at shoulder level, shook his head.

"Cain't do it. It's chained to th' seat."

"Get up there and get it, Barron," Jake Gibson snarled. "We gotta get outa here!"

At the sound of Barron's name, Alan Jensen stiffened, suddenly paying attention to the man who was climbing the wheel of the coach to reach the seat. He looked at this individual carefully. Same height, same build. It could be Jim Barron!

As the driver cowered, fearing a ricochet, the man called Barron aimed at the heavy iron padlock that held the chain around the box. Bits of blasted iron whirled into the dust of the trail below and the man grabbed the box, tossing it to the ground. As he started to climb down, Jake Gibson turned his gun on Alan Jensen.

"I oughta gut—shoot you for what you tried. Get back in th' coach and outa my sight!"

Hurriedly, the agency head clambered back in the coach, leaving his sixgun lying in the dust. In spite of the threat he had just heard, he squinted against the afternoon sun to inspect the man he had heard called Barron.

"Okay," Gibson shouted. "Get this rig outa here!" He fired a shot in the air to emphasize his order. The driver grabbed the reins and slapped them against the backs of his four-horse team, starting them off at a fast trot, then breaking into a gallop.

"You think that driver heard me call you Barron?" Gibson wanted to know, as he aimed at the lock on the box, shattering it with a single shot.

"It was loud enough," Mitch told him, pulling down his mask and grinning. "Th' little guy heard it, too. Fact is, he acted sorta strange when he heard th' name. Face turned white. But I still don't know what this is all about."

Gibson offered him a pitying look. "When that driver and th' passenger tell about Barron bein' in on th' holdup, there'll be a new reward posted on him. And we'll collect with a nice, new, righteously killed corpse!"

Mitch and Grits exchanged glances. Gibson's plan was a bit more complicated than either of them liked.

"Maybe it'll work," Mitch admitted grudgingly.

But Jake Gibson wasn't listening. On his knees, he had opened the box and was staring at a collection of neatly arranged red bricks. A string of profanity issued from his lips.

"Looks like Barron and that banker outsmarted us," Mitch ventured. Gibson's attitude of superiority often bothered him. It was nice to be able to turn the knife a little. "He's prob'ly back at th' shack laughin' hisself sick!"

"He won't laugh long," was Gibson's snarling promise. "Let's go back and finish him off."

"You don't have to hurry none, Jake." The voice was quiet and controlled. All three of the outlaws looked around, searching for the source of the statement. Jim Barron was several yards back from the edge of the trail, half concealed in a grove of trees. His hand gripped the sixgun he had taken from Sid. Behind him, the horse he had taken at the shack stood splay-legged, his body and head covered with sweat and lather.

Gibson took all this in. The spent horse would not have lasted another mile. His gun was still in his hand and he started to raise it. Barron thumbed back the hammer on the gun he held. "Drop it, Jake, or I'll drop you!"

The outlaw hesitated for a moment, then seemed to wilt, as he dropped the gun at his feet.

Mitch had stood silent through this new development. Suddenly, he reacted, grabbing for the gun at his waist. A bullet from Barron's gun smashed into his chest. Dropping the gun, a look of amazement flitted across his face as he was driven backward a step or two and landed flat on his back. He coughed once, tried to rise, blood seeping from his mouth. Then he died.

Jim Barron wasn't watching as the gunman died. His eyes were on the other two. He gestured with his gun to Grits, who still sat his horse, hands raised.

"Real easy now. Unbuckle your gun belt and let it slide down." The outlaw reached for the belt with both hands and Barron, walking across the trail, jabbed the gun in his direction. His eyes were on the horseman now. He looked almost as spent as the horse he had nearly run to death.

"One hand," he warned. "Use your left."

As Grits followed Barron's instructions slowly and with great care, Gibson saw his chance. He made a sudden dive for Barron, aided by the element of surprise to slap the gun out of the detective's hand. At the same time, he shouldered the detective against the iron of the wagon rim. Barron felt a rib crack as he tried to fight back, but he was off balance and falling.

Gibson whirled and mounted his horse in a flying leap, driving the steel rowels of his spurs into the animal's flank. Clutching his damaged side with one hand, Barron clawed in the dust until he found his gun. He fired one shot after the fleeing outlaw, who was now seventy yards away. His hand was shaking and he knew before he pulled the trigger that the shot was a waste of lead.

Grits, frightened by what had gone on, simply sat his horse, fearful that Barron would settle on him as his next target. His gun belt was on the ground at his horse's front feet.

"Were you in on that Silver City bank job?" Barron wanted to know, slowly walking toward the horseman. Grits shook his head.

"Not me, mister. Gibson picked me up less'n a week back. Told me I'd come t'be rich real soon." The man still had his hands raised and couldn't conceal his fright. He was also angry at being left to cope with Barron. "What're you gonna do with me?"

"Nothin'," Barron announced after a moment. "I don't have time t'fool with you. Just ride on outa this country and don't come back!"

The would-be outlaw looked at the hard-faced man for a moment, then nodded. Carefully, he lowered his hands to pick up the reins and move back down the trail, keeping his horse at a walk. Barron watched the rider for an instant, then stalked to Mitch's body, where he reclaimed his own hat and sixgun. He mounted his black horse and rode into the brush behind the coach where he had left the skinny, lathered horse he had ridden from the mining shack.

Without dismounting, he leaned down to undo the saddle cinch on the spent horse, dumping the saddle on the ground. A moment later, he stripped the bit from the horse's mouth and tossed the bridle on top of the saddle. The horse tossed its head and started to move away. Barron watched until the animal stopped to graze on a tuft of grass growing in a clear spot. Satisfied that the horse would recover from his punishing run, Jim Barron rode slowly toward Silver City on his black gelding.

Chapter Sixteen

For the first time in roughly a decade—since the end of the last Apache troubles—the stagecoach wobble-wheeled into Silver City with the horses on a dead run. The driver fought his leather lines, sawing at the horse's bits and cursing each horse by name to bring the lathered four-up to a halt. Even with that effort, he overshot the Wells Fargo office by a couple of buildings.

The clatter of hooves had alerted people to the fact that something exciting had happened and a dozen or so townsmen flooded into the street from the saloon, the bank, and the general store. The fact that the shotgun guard was missing from his seat was lost on only a few.

One of the onlookers who had come from the general store was first to reach the coach, looking up at the driver.

"What's th' matter, Cozy. You hurt?"

"No," the driver bellowed. "I'm not hurt, Jeb, but Billy Jordan's plumb dead back down th' trail and we're short a strong box!"

By this time, the lone passenger had gotten out of the coach, satchel in hand. The other hand was tucked into his vest. Close inspection would reveal a badly swollen wrist that had turned blue. Wincing with pain, he dropped his satchel long enough to adjust his derby with his good hand and look up at Jeb, the one who had questioned the driver.

"You're guard's lying in the trail about five miles back," Jenson announced, tone somewhat clinical. He picked up his satchel, again. "I'm pretty sure he's dead, but somebody ought to go pick him up!"

Jeb, who looked like a miner, turned to glare at the little man with the derby hat and the Eastern clothes. "Who're you?" he demanded

"Alan Jensen, president of the Jensen Detective Agency."

"One of your men's around town somewhere. Fellah named Barron. We'd best get him."

Jensen was flustered. There was no way he could come out of this smelling like the proverbial rose. Skunk cabbage would be more like it. He looked around at the citizens who were suddenly staring at him. He heaved a sigh and made the plunge.

"Jim Barron? He's one of them that robbed us! Where's Lem Turner? I need to see him."

"I reckon he's at home. He's taken to havin' a nap on a hot afternoon." Jeb glanced at Jensen's wrist, nodding at it. "Looks like you need t' see th' doctor right quick."

Jensen waved an imperious hand to dismiss the thought. "Not until I see Turner and the sheriff." He took a new breath and raised his voice so others would hear. "I want a posse out looking for Jim Barron immediately. I'm offering a reward for him personally. Five thousand dollars, dead or alive!"

Jeb cocked his head to stare at the newcomer. He scowled. "A reward? For your own man?

Jensen cooled the intensity of his anger and frustration with some difficulty, replacing it with a demeanor of coldness. "Jim Barron is an outlaw. He has also put the Jensen Detective Agency in a totally embarrassing position."

Jeb nodded toward the rear of the stagecoach. "Th' sheriff's office is a block down th' street, mister, but I don't think he's there."

Jeb was right. The sheriff was out serving papers on behalf of the local court, but his deputy was quick to agree a posse should be mounted up. Jim Barron was the only one of the robbers for whom there had been positive identification. If they caught him, Alan Jensen insisted, they could surely force him to identify the others.

In less than forty minutes, a six-man posse led by the deputy rode out of town. Behind them was a flat-bed wagon that would be used by the town's mortician to bring in the body of the dead shotgun guard. He didn't know it then, but his return load also would carry the dead gun hand, Mitch.

Hidden between two buildings, Jake Gibson watched the posse ride down the street in the direction of the holdup. He licked his lips nervously, as he stepped out onto the board sidewalk and watched the little man who had been in the coach moving carefully down the other side of the street. He had one hand tucked into his vest and was obviously in some sort of pain. The man turned into the office of the town's one doctor, and Gibson could not suppress a scowl. Breaking the interfering fool's wrist had not been enough. He should have killed the pompous little clown while he had the chance.

There was some satisfaction, though, in being reasonably certain the man could not identify him. Still, the smartest thing he could do would be to close things down and get out of town fast!

Gibson had left his horse tied behind the Scarlet Lily before he had edged between the buildings to the sidewalk. There was a back entrance to the saloon, but he was aware that it led to Rita Lansworth's office and she always kept it locked.

Watching both sides of the street but trying not to turn his head in doing so, Jake Gibson made it to the swinging doors of the saloon and edged into the quiet, semi-dark interior. He stopped and carefully surveyed the room. The relief bartender was on duty and there was no sign of Charlie Reese. Carl Lee, head buried in his folded arms, was asleep at his poker table. A nearly empty bottle and a glass were in front of him. Rita came out of the office, not noticing Gibson standing beside the door at first. She frowned as she finally saw him.

"What's happening? What's all the excitement up the street?" she wanted to know. She glanced around the empty room. "Where is everyone?"

Gibson shook his head, advancing to the bar and signaling Zeke, the relief man. "I don't know," he growled, answering Rita. "Just some riders goin' down th' street."

He motioned to the back bar, looking at Zeke. "Bourbon. I'll take th' bottle."

The bottle and a glass were shoved across the counter in his direction. Zeke maintained a neutral expression, but his manner indicated he did not like waiting on the man. Gibson ignored him and Rita, as he glanced about the room, then chose a blind corner just inside the swinging doors.

Rita watched Gibson for a moment, then turned toward the table where Carl Lee was sprawled in sleep. She glanced at the bald bartender.

"How long has he been there like that?" she wanted to know. Zeke offered a shrug.

"He was like that when I come in t'relieve Charlie," he replied, passing along the blame. "Maybe he shoulda woke him up."

"Where's Charlie?" the woman demanded, frowning.

"Said he had personal business to take care of. Said he'd work for me t'night." He had seen Rita Lansworth angry just once and it hadn't been pleasant. He didn't want her sore at him. He couldn't help heaving a sigh of relief, as she stalked between the tables to where Carl was asleep.

The conversation had been used as cover by Jake Gibson to slip his sixgun from his holster and tuck it between his legs, butt resting with one hand on it, finger near the trigger. In spite of her own problems and growing anger, Rita had seen the veiled move. The observation only caused her scowl to deepen, as she grabbed the gambler roughly by the shoulder and shook him.

"Carl! Wake up!" she ordered sternly. "I want you to hear me!"

The reply was a slight stirring of Lee's upper body and mumbled words that meant nothing to her. She shook him once more, being rougher than the first time. This time, her voice was angry.

"This is a place of business," she snarled, grabbing the back of Lee's coat and pulling him partially erect. She slapped him across the face several times, as she continued. "This is no place for you to lay around drunk!"

Her open hand beating a tattoo on his cheeks and mouth caused Carl Lee to open his eyes, then raise a hand to ward off her blows.

"M'not drunk," he answered. "I jus' don't feel well." He started to lower his head, again, but she grabbed his hair to pull him erect. He looked at her through hazy, tortured eyes.

"I tol' you. I'm sick," he insisted, his words half moaned.

"I need to talk to you." She was still angry, but a pleading note had entered her tone. "It's important! In the office! Please!"

She caught movement beyond the swinging doors and heard hard heels hesitate on the board sidewalk outside. Rita also saw Jake Gibson, slumped in the chair in the dark corner, stiffen, sitting up straighter, watching. An instant later, a cowboy she didn't know walked through the doors, headed for the bar. Gibson, accepting the fact that the man was no threat, relaxed, heaving a nervous sigh.

Rita looked down at Carl Lee, her expression no longer angry. It was simply a show of sadness. She shook her head.

"You're hopeless, Carl." She turned and strode across the floor to her office, closing the door. Carl Lee sat for a moment, looking slowly around the room through whiskey-fogged eyes. Finally, he pushed himself erect and picked up the bottle from the table. He measured the contents with his eyes, seemed to decide that the task of tilting it was not worthy of effort and put it down. Like an old man, he tottered toward the door Rita had closed behind her. Wondering what had gotten into Carl, Zeke watched, frowning disapproval. He offered a shake of his head, as Lee tried the door-knob. Finding it unlocked, he pushed his way into the office. The cowboy at the bar paid no attention, waiting patiently to be served, but Jake Gibson had watched the gambler through narrowed eyes as he had half—stumbled across the room.

In her office, Rita was unlocking her back door as Carl entered. He reached out to grab the back of a chair for support. She had turned at the sound of the door closing, still scowling.

"Whass alla trouble?" Lee wanted to know. The girl had been on the point of going to find the sheriff her-self. Now she stepped closer to him, attempting to judge his capabilities. After an instant, she made her decision.

"Carl," she said slowly, hoping he would under-stand, "There is going to be big trouble here. I want you to go out this back door and find the sheriff. Bring him here."

The gambler glanced at the door to the barroom, then turned back to her, shaking his head. "Whatcha talkin' about?" he demanded.

Rita maintained her calm appearance with an effort.

Carl was wasting valuable time. "Jack Gibson is sitting out there in a corner with a hidden gun in his hand. He's going to kill someone!"

The gambler loosed his hold on the back of the chair and nearly fell, as he turned toward the barroom door intent on taking a look. Rita reached out to grab his shoulder.

"Please, Carl. Get the sheriff!"

Carl Lee shrugged and turned once again toward the door.

"No, Carl. You have to find him!" Still hanging onto the shoulder of his coat, she spun the gambler about, pointing him toward the rear door. Seeming to surrender to her demands, he stumbled to the door and opened it. An instant later, he was staggering down the alley past the horse that Gibson had left tied there.

Rita Lansworth watched him for a moment, making certain he was headed in the right direction and hoping he didn't pass out on the way. She closed the door, leaving it unlocked and turned to her desk. She opened the top drawer and drew out an object wrapped in an oily towel. Laying it on the desk, she slowly undid the folds to reveal a Navy Colt, a relic of her father's service in the Civil War.

Her father had maintained a reputation as a peaceful man and had not allowed any of his employees to carry guns in the saloon. What they wanted to do in the street on their own time was not his business, but what they did under his roof was. Hidden under the bar, however, there had always been—and still was—an Irish club and a sawed-off double-barreled shotgun of uncertain vintage. According to those who had known him while she was away at school, her father had never been forced to resort to the shotgun or any other firearm. A few times, she had been told, he had whaled about with the heavy oak shillelagh to break up fights and save his saloon from being wrecked.

Rita Lansworth had never fired a gun. She stared at the odd-looking Navy Colt, not aware that firing it required that percussion caps must be mounted on the teats extending from the six chambers. She didn't know whether it was loaded, either.

After a moment, she wrapped the gun again in the towel and put it back in the drawer. There was nothing she could do but wait to see what happened, who got killed. For perhaps the first time in her life, she felt totally helpless. Part of that feeling was generated by wondering where Jim Barron might be and whether he was Jake Gibson's planned target.

Worse was the feeling that she knew there was nothing she could do to stop the violence!

Chapter Seventeen

In spite of Rita Lansworth's doubts, Carl Lee managed to make it through the alley until he came to the
cross—street closest to the sheriff's office. He stood
there in the hot afternoon sun, sweating profusely. He
lowered his head and sniffed, imagining he could
smell the alcohol escaping from his pores.

For a long moment, he considered abandoning the
mission and returning to the relative coolness of the
bar, but some guidance out of his childhood training
crept into his thinking. As a youngster, it had been
impressed upon him that "one does not make a fool
of himself in public." He had done that already and
returning to the bar would only make him look more
the fool.

His head was throbbing, but Carl Lee could not help

a wry chuckle from squeezing between his dry lips. He'd already done that, getting drunk and falling all over himself. Maybe it had been the shock of having Rita slap his face that had caused him to be suddenly willing to face at least a little bit of reality.

He chuckled again. An alley in the bright summer sun was no place to get philosophical. He suddenly felt his stomach rebel against the booze, the sun and the exercise. He propped himself against the nearest building to vomit, the smell of liquor mixed with gall enough to cause a repeat performance. Done, he stepped aside and leaned against the building for several minutes, breathing heavily. He knew he had done something right. He felt more himself. Yes, he thought ironically, ready to fulfill Rita's assigned mission: Find the sheriff!

Slumped wearily in the saddle, Jim Barron was nearing the edge of Silver City. He had followed the range of hills flanking the trail and had seen the posse riding hell—bent—for—leather toward the crime scene. That had caused a twisted grin to shape his lips, but he did not hurry the tired gelding.

Barron was tired too, and hungry. It had been nearly twenty-four hours since he had eaten and he doubted that his horse had been treated any better. It was obvious the animal had been ridden hard with little regard by the outlaw, Mitch. The detective, in his years of chasing badmen, had come to realize that most of them didn't know much about horses or, at least, about caring for them. Because a horse was big, they thought it should be able to go on forever. They failed to realize that the weakest part of a horse's body was its legs. They were thin and complicated, having to support more than a thousand pounds of the animal's own weight, plus a saddle and the rider. Others might realize a horse's shortcomings, but their attitude was "use it up. I can always get another." At the opposite extreme, the U.S. Cavalry had a spoken policy: "Try never to run a horse farther than you'd run yourself." That statement also covered the bank detective's personal code.

That was only one of series of subjects that had entered Jim Barron's meandering, disconnected thinking as he had ridden away from the holdup scene. He had taken a longer route, because he knew there would be people coming to the robbery scene, and he didn't want to waste time with discussion or explanations. He had also figured out that with Mitch wearing his hat, carrying his gun and riding his horse, he had been set up very effectively.

Jim Barron did not want to admit it, but nonetheless he had begun to wonder whether he had wasted a good deal of his life. Early on, doing unpleasant jobs had been a means of feeding himself and Tim Mathis. But after capturing his first two bandits and being hired by Alan Jensen, life had taken on a different meaning. Every robbery and every robber became a personal challenge and he followed the trail until the outlaws were either captured or slain.

During those later years behind the walls at Fort Madison, he'd had plenty of time to think about all that, wondering why he had felt that way. It had to be something to do with being the victor, besting another human being in a game of life and death. He had come to accept his past as that—a big game, with him on one side, the lawless on the other—but he still did not understand the why of that feeling. That lack had frustrated him for the last two years of his imprisonment.

He wondered, too, why he had been so ready to sign on with Alan Jensen and come to New Mexico to find his brother's killer. Was that more of the same game or should it be thought of in the light of a personal score to be settled? Rocking along to the gait of the plodding gelding, Barron shook his head. He didn't know.

Over all of those years, and especially the prison years, he had maintained the ability to display a poker face, never to let anyone know exactly what he was thinking or how he felt. A few times, when working a job with Tim during the latter's training period, he had let a little of himself show.

He remembered one night in a willow grove on a creek with a long-forgotten name, when Tim had asked whether he ever intended to get married. Barron's answer had been a decided negative.

"You're the last of the Barron line, Jim," Tim had

said quietly. "You don't think about having children to carry on your name?"

"A name's not important," Barron had declared. "It's what you do that counts." He had poured the dregs from the coffee pot to put out their fire, then huddled in his blankets. Years later, in Fort Madison, he had recalled the puzzled look on Tim's face at what he had said.

And he had awakened many times during those last two years, wondering what he really had meant. In fact, he had come to realize that he did want to marry, he did want children and he did want to hang up his gun. There was not much future for a fifty- or sixty-year-old detective. That was evidenced by the fact that most of them were dead before they reached that age.

At the edge of town, Barron drew rein to look down the main street. He was looking for the horse on which Jake Gibson had been mounted as he had raced away from the holdup scene. He saw no sign of the horse. In fact, there was only one horse on the street. It was tied in front of the Scarlet Lily, but it wasn't Gibson's scrubby blue roan.

Riding down the street, Barron turned in at the livery stable to look over his stalls and the adjoining corral. No luck. He shook his head, then cut back from the street to follow the alley behind the row of business establishments. He was not surprised when he saw Gibson's spent roan behind the saloon, head dropping and back hunched against the tight cinch. Barron sat his horse, considering the situation, eyes slitted against the late afternoon sun that filtered between two of the structures. The easy thing would be to hide his horse and take up a post where he could wait for Gibson to return for his mount.

Several blocks away, Carl Lee was pounding on the door of the sheriff's office. He had tried the doorknob, but the door was locked. He moved to the side and tried to look through the window that looked out on the street, but it was covered by a pulled shade.

"Something wrong?" the voice asked behind him and Carl Lee whirled, frightened simply at finding he was not alone. Charlie Reese was wearing a suit and looked more like a businessman than a working bartender. Lee heaved a sigh, exhaling loudly.

"Jake Gibson's over in the salon nursing a gun in his lap," Lee told him rapidly. "Rita wants to stop any trouble before it gets started, but he's ready for a shootout." He paused for a hurried breath. "You seen the sheriff?"

Reese shook his head, frowning. "I just got back into town. Was out lookin' at a ranch I might buy."

Lee looked at him as though not understanding. Reese offered him a thin smile.

"You know. Get outa th' bar business. No place for a tired, old man."

"Well, we have to find him," Lee decided for the both of them. "I'll check up the street. The general store and the restaurant. You want to look down around the livery stable?"

"Sure. Right now," Charlie Reese offered agreeably, and started toward the livery barn positioned two blocks away. Lee, his gait now relatively steady, plodded in the opposite direction.

In the bar, the lone cowboy had finished his drink. Finding that Zeke was not one for conversation and was more interested in watching the door to Rita's office, he left money on the bar and strode toward the entrance. Sweeping both of the louvered batwing doors aside, he turned down the sidewalk, not seeing Jim Barron crouched beside the door frame.

His hand on his holstered gun, Barron slowly looked over the top of the nearest door. The mirror that Rita's father had imported from St. Louis a section at a time and as money allowed ran the full length of the bar. Surveying the room, lighted now by the lowering sun casting rays over the doors, Jim Barron spotted Jake Gibson at the corner table. Had the outlaw not had his head tilted back for a drink from the shot glass, he might well have noticed the shadow of Barron's head darkening the top of one of the tables. Barron noted the giveaway, though, and quickly withdrew.

The detective paused for a moment, looking up and down the street. It was empty. He needed a distraction, but there were no people, no horses. Finally, Barron stood and retreated several yards down the wall to raise one foot and buckle one spur. Then, he repeated the effort with the other spur. He gripped them tightly so the rowels would not rattle and give him away, then tiptoed back to the edge of the door.

Hesitating only a moment, he whirled and hurled the tangled spurs in an overhand throw, clearing the tops of the swinging doors. The bundled iron and leather flew across the room and smashed a bottle of whiskey on the back bar. Zeke, conditioned by violence in numerous Western saloons, immediately dropped behind the bar to avoid becoming a target.

Jake Gibson displayed his fear and nervousness by leaping to his feet, tipping over the table and taking several steps toward the center of the room, staring at the broken bottle. The sixgun was in his hand and he suddenly recognized a trap. As he started to turn toward the doors, Jim Barron rocketed between them, diving for the outlaw. With a vicious slash of his hand, he sent the gunman's revolver skidding across the floor.

Gibson rolled away from Barron's hold, springing to his feet. Tired, the detective was slower and rose in time to have Gibson dive at him. He managed to turn away and, at the same time, aim a telling kick at the outlaw's ribs.

Both men were on their feet suddenly, swinging punches made less effective by their wildness. An uppercut drove Barron back to fall across the table where Carl Lee had left the bottle and shot glass. Realizing his momentary advantage, Gibson skidded across the floor, hand outstretched for his sixgun that was canted against the bottom of the bar.

Barron's reaction was to grab up the bottle he found within reach and hurl it. The quart container of brown glass broke on the gun metal as Gibson's hand closed around it. Blood gushed from the outlaw's wrist and he was unable to hold on to the sixgun.

Scrambling to his feet, Barron used all the strength he could summon to wade into the outlaw, dragging him to his feet, while blood from the slashed wrist splashed across both of them. With Gibson backed against the bar and unable to defend himself, the detective pounded him unmercifully. As the unconscious outlaw slid to the floor, Barron saw Rita standing in the office doorway, horrified at what she had been watching.

Zeke came up from behind the bar slowly, surveying the room. Rita stared at him accusingly. "Why didn't you do something?" she demanded.

Zeke shook his head. "Not me, ma'am. I didn't know whose side I was s'posed to be on!"

Barron wiped his face with his sleeve, then looked at Rita. "Get some rags. We've got t' tie off that cut b'fore he bleeds to death!"

Rita didn't move, but Zeke reached beneath the bar to extend a handful of bar towels. Nodding thanks, Barron bent painfully to tie one of the lengths of cloth around Gibson's wrist and twist it to stop the flow of blood. He glanced at the bartender.

"Zeke, go round up the doc. We've got some business for him. Hurry!" The bartender glanced at Rita, and she nodded, causing him to strip off his apron and head for the door. As he left, the woman walked over to stare down at Gibson, who was beginning to stir. Then she scowled at Barron.

"What right do you have to come in here and tear up my place?" she demanded. Barron offered her his own scowl.

"I'm a bank detective. I suppose you gave this man permission t'sit here quietly and shoot me!"

Rita offered a strangled laugh. "You're an outlaw. There's a price on your head!"

Barron cast her a strange look, then reached down to grab Gibson by the front of his shirt. There was the sound of tearing cloth as he raised the outlaw to his feet. He danced him backward until Gibson was shoved into a chair. Barron bent over him.

"Who gives the orders, Gibson?" His voice was demanding, but the outlaw only grabbed his torn wrist, nursing it, staring at the top of the bar mirror.

"I don't know what you're talkin' about."

Barron straightened and offered a shrug, while Rita stood looking on, her face showing a series of emotions, none of them joy.

"Okay. Play it that way. You'll be th' one th' State

of New Mexico walks up th' gallows stairs by your lonesome."

A hint of fear crept into the outlaw's eyes to dilute his stubborn expression. He shook his head. "You can't hang me. You can't prove nothin'."

"My brother was killed in that last bank robbery and the guard was murdered today." Barron offered a positive nod of his head. "You'll hang."

Gibson could not hide the panic that spread across his features. "I'm not hangin' for someone else," he declared. "I ain't shot nobody."

"Talk!" Barron ordered, grinding out the single word.

As Gibson opened his mouth, there was a single shot and the outlaw slumped forward to fall off the chair.

Chapter Eighteen

Charlie Reese stood in the doorway, a small pistol in his hand. Barron automatically classified it as a Colt-made .41 caliber Derringer, which had been introduced the previous year, in 1886. The compact little gun boasted chrome plating and diminutive black grips. It had been marketed initially as a defense tool for businessmen who might be called upon to conduct some of their affairs in rough areas. In reality, it had become the hideout weapon for professional gamblers who thought they might be accused of cheating.

The gun had two barrels, one stacked atop the other, which meant the second shot was still ready in Reese's pistol. Barron realized that his knowledge of the little handgun's capabilities made it no less deadly.

Apparently, Reese had entered some time during the

fight, but Barron certainly had not noticed him. It appeared no one else had either. The big man who stood before them now was not the affable, easy-going bartender they all thought they knew. Charlie Reese's eyes were narrowed and nervous perspiration had darkened his collar. There was a sense of desperation about him that was tempered by a look of cool calculation.

"Everyone! Get your hands up!" Charlie Reese advanced slowly to face Barron, who had followed the order like the others. The bartender glared into the detective's alert eyes.

"I'd have saved a lotta trouble if I'd just plugged you th' other night at Turner's."

"You were th' one listenin' at th' window," Barron accused.

"Unbuckle your gun belt and let it drop," Reese demanded, jamming the derringer forward as a signal for immediate action. Slowly, Barron reached across his body with his left hand and unbuckled the belt, keeping the other hand at shoulder level. The gun belt thudded to the floor with its holstered sixgun.

The Derringer still leveled at Barron's belly, Reese side-stepped him and grabbed Rita roughly by the arm. She struggled, but he twisted her arm behind her back, bringing a cry of pain. Slowly, he began to back toward Rita's office.

"Just come along with me, Rita," he growled. "No one's gonna take a chance on shootin' a woman."

In spite of the pain Reese was creating, Rita twisted again, trying to get away. Barron took a step forward, starting to lower his hands. Reese jammed the little pistol in his direction, again.

"Easy!" In the beginning, Charlie Reese had seemed somewhat uncertain. Now, however, his expression had become vicious, veiling his fear. Obviously, things had not gone as planned. "I'll blow your belt buckle through your backbone, Barron. I'm savin' this second barrel just for you."

Barron had his hands back up, palms level with his shoulders, but his expression had become equally as harsh as Reese's.

"I'm gonna get you yet, Charlie." Barron's voice was gutteral with emotion. "Make no mistake. I'll come for you!"

Holding the girl in front of him, Charlie raised the Derringer with a snarl. The bartender did not realize that the door behind him had opened slowly and Carl Lee had taken in the scene. Barron was surprised, but didn't let it show in his face. Warned perhaps by Barron's seeming concentration on a spot somewhere to his rear, Charlie whirled toward the office door. In the same moment, Rita managed to wrench free, deliberately falling to the floor.

Carl Lee launched himself from his position in the doorway, meeting Reese head-on, as the latter turned. The two struggled, the outlaw leader attempting to bring the Derringer into play, while Lee sought to control it. As they wrestled, the stronger Reese managed to get the little gun down between them. There was an explosion muffled somewhat by the two close-pressed bodies. Carl Lee's body went limp and Reese stepped back, allowing the gambler to fall as he whirled toward Jim Barron, once more extending the little over/under gun in obvious threat.

Reese pulled the trigger and there was a snapping sound as the firing pin fell on an empty cartridge. Desperate, he pulled the trigger again. Both bullets had been used. With a grim smile, Barron bent to pull the sixgun from his grounded holster. Standing erect, he leveled the gun at Charlie Reese, who dropped the now useless weapon and began to back away. Suddenly panicked, he seemed close to tears, as Barron advanced on him.

"I didn't tell 'em to kill anyone," he mumbled, spittle issuing from a corner of his mouth. "It was Mitch. He was th' one! He likes killin'!"

Reese came to a halt, backed now against the wall. Behind the bar, Zeke had finally taken action and had the antique shotgun leveled across the expanse of wood, pointing it at Reese.

Barron was within five feet of Reese, when he thumbed back the hammer on his Colt revolver. Slumped against the wall, nowhere to go, Reese reached up to cover his eyes with his hands. When he spoke, he cringed, his voice only a hoarse whisper.

"Don't shoot! For God's sake, Barron! Please! Don't!"

Chapter Nineteen

The session in the Sheriff Ord's office to sort things out ran until well after midnight. Earlier, the town mortician had been busy gathering up corpses around the county. No sooner had he returned to town with the bodies of the slain shotgun guard and the bandit identified as Troy Mitchell, than he had been called to the saloon. Rita had closed the Scarlet Lily, but that was where the mortician found the bodies of Carl Lee and Jake Gibson. He was also the Grant County coroner, but the meeting was well under way by the time he arrived.

He labeled the deaths of the shotgun guard and Carl Lee as murder and the timely passing of both Mitch and Gibson as receiving "their just desserts." That brought him a raised eyebrow from the sheriff and the banker, and the appointed official quickly looked into the legal tome covering such events. He finally listed the demise of the two gunmen as "death by misadventure."

Others gathered in the office were Sheriff Ord, Lem Turner, Alan Jensen and Jim Barron. Jensen sat in a corner and listened, piqued at not being included in most of the conversation and pretending not to be surprised as he learned what had really happened.

It turned out he was the outsider. Ord, Turner and Barron had all been a part of the plan to smoke out the bank bandits. Actually, the gold from the Deming bank had been on the coach. Instead of the strongbox, the pieces from the Denver mint had been packed in buckskin bags that were hidden under the seat on which Alan Jensen had ridden into town!

Jensen looked pained when he heard this and squirmed when the sheriff glanced at him and chuckled. Barron simply ignored him. The old Iowa reward poster had been planted deliberately to get Barron an in with the gang. The operation had been a success except for the death of the shotgun guard.

"That was out-and-out murder," Alan Jensen put in. Other than the driver, he was the only witness. "He just rode up and shot the man twice. I heard it. He was laughing! That Mitch enjoyed watching people die!" No one had any other comment.

The door leading to the cellblock stood open and there was no doubt that Charlie Reese could hear all that was said, but there was no sound from him. Soon after he had been jailed, he had asked for a Bible and had read it until dark.

Once Reese had been jailed, the sheriff had obtained a search warrant from the local judge. He and Barron had found more than $18,000 of the bank robbery loot tucked away in Charlie's suitcase shoved under his bed at the Miner's Rest. He had admitted that the rest of the money had been used to pay off Gibson and his gang.

"Well, I guess I'm ready for a run on the bank, if it's going to happen," Lem Turner stated as the meeting broke up.

The sheriff shook his head. "When word gets out in th' mornin' that you got back mosta th' loot, I don't expect that to be a problem."

Alan Jensen tried to walk to the hotel with Barron, but the detective had stalked away from him, lengthening a stride that the little man could not match.

In spite of the hour, Barron was able to talk the hotel manager into heating enough water for him take a bath in his room, using half of a whiskey barrel that served occupants of the top—floor rooms as a tub.

Clean and scrubbed, he slipped between the sheets in the nude. One of his last thoughts was that he would have to claim the rest of his laundry from the Widow Stern. His final thought, as sleep swept over his weariness like a balm, was of Rita. He wondered where she was and what she was doing. He doubted that she would ever fully recover from her ordeal and having Carl Lee shot down in front of her.

The weather the next morning was cooler than it had been in weeks. It had the promise of a nice day, Jim Barron noted as he saddled his horse at the livery stable and tied on his saddlebags and bedroll. He had reclaimed his laundry early and it was tucked in the bags. He was dressed in the black shirt and trousers he had worn when he rode into town. He had taken a moment to rub his Stetson with a towel in the hotel room, getting rid of most of the dust, then had made a swipe across his black boots with the same cloth.

Making his morning inspection, the livery operator sauntered past the stalls and paused as he saw what Barron was doing. He reached out to rub the gelding's nose.

"Hate t'see you take him away, Mister Barron. I been gettin' mighty fond of this animal."

Barron allowed himself a quiet smile. "I'm kinda fond of him myself."

The liveryman was frowning, staring at the detective's waist. "You ain't ridin' outa here unarmed, are you?"

Barron offered a nod, reaching up to tap one of the saddlebags. "Yep. I'm goin' to hang that Peacemaker on a nail and maybe clean it twice a year."

"Jim! Jim Barron!" Alan Jensen was framed in the double doorway at the front of the barn. He peered into the shadows, then started down the straw-littered passageway between the rows of stalls. Barron had paused, scowling, as he stared at the little man.

Jensen finally saw Barron and hurried to face him. The livery operator saw the expression on Barron's face and quietly turned to walk away. As Jensen halted before him, Barron simply continued to stare at him. The other man tried to force a grin.

"I've been looking all over town for you, Jim. We have to talk."

Barron said nothing, staring at him hard-eyed, waiting for him to continue.

"I need men like you, Jim. You did a fine job here, rounding up this gang. How about it? You'll be my chief investigator, again."

Barron turned his back on the man, shaking his head. He began to retie the bedroll behind his saddle. "I don't think so, Al."

Jensen frowned at the other's back. "Why not? There'll be a good raise."

Barron turned back to stare coldly into Alan Jensen's eyes. "You tried to feed me to th' wolves, again, Al. Didn't trust me t'handle this alone and you had t'mess it up!"

Jensen's expression became defensive. "Jim, I didn't."

Interrupting, Barron's tone suddenly was harsh with anger. "You nearly got me killed, Al, sendin' that posse after me. Without any kind of real proof, you thought I'd been one of th' robbers. You had t'jumped right into it!."

"It was a mistake, Jim. I can make it up to you."

Barron shook his head, still scowling. "Don't try to make up anything to me, Jensen. Make it up to Tim Mathis. Go up on the hill and look at his grave. Buy him a decent marker. If you don't do that much for him, I'll start tellin' your bankers how you treat your people. I'll be spreadin' that word everywhere I go!"

Barron grabbed his horse's reins and turned. Jenson, with an upraised, placating hand, tried to block his way. Barron simply shouldered him aside. The little man had to scuttle backward to avoid being walked on by the big gelding.

Barron led the horse into the street and paused as he saw Rita Lansworth climbing into a buggy that had been waiting. He had noticed the horse tied to the corral fence as he had entered the barn, sure it was the same horse she'd driven to the cemetery the day of their picnic.

Leading the black, Barron walked over to halt beside her as she settled herself on the seat. If she had seen him, she didn't show it.

"Good morning," he said quietly. "You're out and about mighty early."

Rita looked down at him from the seat, face a reflection of her sadness. "I'm going up to the cemetery to pick out a plot for Carl."

Barron nodded his understanding. "Down underneath, I think he was a decent enough man. I think he tried to warn me outa th' country th' other day by shootin' in my direction."

"I know. He had so much to offer," she said, offering a slow nod, "but so far to go."

For an instant, neither spoke. Finally, Barron glanced at his horse. "If you don't mind, I'll ride up there with you. I want to say goodbye to my brother."

The woman looked at him, judging, before she spoke. "You could use a bit of peace and quiet yourself. I have breakfast in my basket. Enough for both of us. Why don't you come along to the creek with me?"

The stable operator had come out to see that everything was proper with the rental buggy. He paused, as Jim Barron offered a wide smile, looking up at Rita.

"I wondered whether you were going to ask me," he admitted. She laughed, as he handed his horse's reins to the stableman.

"Here. Put him back in the stall and toss him some hay. I'll be back."

Quickly, he climbed into the buggy and took the lines from Rita's hands. He slapped the horse on its back with the loose lengths of leather, starting him ambling down the street.

The stableman watched as the pair drove away, laughter sounding in their wake. Finally, he heaved a sigh and looked at the big black.

"Come on, horse. Looks like your gonna be around here a long while."

The gelding tossed his head in what seemed to be agreement, then stepped off beside the man with no indication of reluctance.